"I WANTED TO TALK . . . THAT'S ALL."

She clutched her dusting cloth tightly. "I thanked you already for saving me. You said you wanted nothing for paying my hospital fee. Have you changed your mind?" *Because I'm not for sale . . . Not, not, not . . .*

"*Nee, sei se gut*—I mean, no, I haven't."

"Why," she exclaimed, studying him more carefully, "you're Amish . . ."

Stephen swallowed and nodded. "Yeah, but I guess I don't spread that around so much."

"Where is your Amish community?"

"You—you know about the Amish?"

She smiled faintly, and he felt like warmed syrup was running down his spine at the endearing glimpse of her pearl white teeth. "When I was—when I was traveling here, the train had a stopover for a few hours at a town called Renew. I was sort of hungry, and a kind Amish woman had a small stand at the depot. She seemed to know that I didn't have much money, and she gave me a cheese sandwich and a ripe red tomato to eat."

She looked back to the cleaning rag she held, seemingly embarrassed by her torrent of speech, and he wanted to *geh* round the bed and touch her, comfort her. But he stood still and cleared his throat. "I come from a place called Ice Mountain."

An Amish Match
ON ICE MOUNTAIN

KELLY LONG

ZEBRA BOOKS
KENSINGTON PUBLISHING CORP.

http://www.kensingtonbooks.com

ZEBRA BOOKS are published by

Kensington Publishing Corp.
119 West 40th Street
New York, NY 10018

All Kensington titles, imprints, and distributed lines are available at special quantity discounts for bulk purchases for sales promotion, premiums, fund-raising, educational, or institutional use.

Special book excerpts or customized printings can also be created to fit specific needs. For details, write or phone the office of the Kensington Sales Manager: Attn.: Sales Department. Kensington Publishing Corp., 119 West 40th Street, New York, NY 10018. Phone: 1-800-221-2647.

First Printing: December 2018
ISBN-13: 978-1-4201-4127-6
ISBN-10: 1-4201-4127-9

eISBN-13: 978-1-4201-4128-3
eISBN-10: 1-4201-4128-7

10 9 8 7 6 5 4 3 2 1

Printed in the United States of America

For Jordan—who sees . . .

PART I

COUDERSPORT, PA, 1958

Chapter One

Stephen Lambert lay on his back in the inky darkness and tried to block out the raucous sounds coming from the next room.

The guys were entertaining a bunch of girls from town, and there was plenty of loud music and laughter.

Great, Stephen thought. *How am I ever going to get any sleep with all that commotion going on in the break room?*

The girls were probably from the local bawdy house, and the party was a world away from anything he'd ever known growing up in the little Amish community of Ice Mountain.

He turned on his side and grabbed his pillow, ramming it over his head. He knew it was wrong, but he was infinitely grateful when the alarm bell rang, clanging against any forthcoming sounds he might have heard.

He swung his legs over the side of the cot, pulled up his suspenders, and slid on his waterproof boots.

He ran down the hallway, falling into line with the other firefighters until they reached the engine room.

Stephen was number seven, and he methodically pulled on the heavy coat and plastic hat, tightened the chin strap, and turned toward the truck, only to bump into Mike, the chief.

Mike was a different man when he wasn't romancing some local girl, Stephen thought. This Mike barked concise orders and soon had everyone on the engine in proper position, including the station's wolf dog, Midnight.

Coudersport was a small but bustling logging and coal town deep in the mountains of Pennsylvania. Because the town had grown up practically overnight, a lot of the local structures were not built well, and even some of the nicer buildings could become a fireman's nightmare.

The fire engine, Old Betsy, roared down the main street of town, following the dark plume of smoke that rose against the moonlit sky. Their destination was a boardinghouse on the wrong side of town—a neighborhood where the poor congregated, sometimes living on the streets despite the cold.

The boardinghouse had gone up like kindling, and the false front of the building had already half collapsed, spewing flames out into the late spring air.

Stephen began to pray automatically; maybe it was something to do with being Amish, but it was natural for him to beg *Gott* for mercy for his crew friends and those inside.

The engine roared to a stop, and Mike began to shout at onlookers to get out of the way. Stephen saw Midnight take up his post, prowling the perimeter of the building, looking for anyone in need. Other crew members were running out the hoses while Stephen and two other men took up ladders and tried to find a viable position.

It was strange, but after a few fires, Stephen had begun to be able to separate sounds in his head—the cries of onlookers versus the screams of those inside. And now he heard it. A frantic female cry for help, coming from the second floor. His praying escalated as he grabbed the longer of the two metal ladders and moved toward the heat.

Joe, Stephen's big friend, shook his helmeted head. "Too risky, Steve. That whole false front is goin' to go any second!"

"I'll be down fast. You know I will!" Stephen ignored his friend's warnings and found a place near the far right of the structure that would allow him to get close to the window frame.

He could see her now, her long red hair hanging from the sill. Her young face looked terrified and sooty. He went up the ladder without fear, wishing for about the tenth time since starting this job that his company could afford a fancy breathing apparatus for each member of the crew. As it was, the only protection he had against smoke inhalation was a damp neckerchief tied around his mouth and nose.

The girl saw him and ducked down inside the sill. It was a common enough reaction; victims of fire were often uncertain when rescue was near.

"Stand up!" he shouted. "Stand up."

Mercifully, the girl obeyed. He could tell now that she was older than he'd thought, but all of this went through his head in a rush as he felt the water pressure from the hose spray his legs and back. There couldn't be much time if they were wetting him down from below.

The girl's frantic gaze locked with his. "All right." He nodded. "You're going to have to jump!"

Ella Nichols stared in horror at the fireman. His black hat and yellow coat seemed to waver in the heat of the fire.

"I can't jump," she screamed back at him, terrified at the thought of falling.

"I'll catch you. You won't fall—I promise!"

Ella thought of how much easier her life might be if she simply sank to the floor and gave up. But then she thought of the unborn child she was carrying and straightened her spine. She slung one leg over the windowsill, which seemed hot even to the touch.

She looked down and felt a wave of nausea.

"Don't look down!" he ordered, apparently watching her every move.

"All right!" She cautiously eased her other leg out, then grabbed the sill with her fingernails as a whoosh of flames flared up behind her.

"Jump when I tell you. On three."

He extended his arms, somehow balancing on the high, swaying ladder with only his legs for support.

"One!"

I'm going to die.

"Two!"

I don't want this baby to die.

"Three!!!"

She closed her eyes and jumped . . .

She was conscious of hitting a chest as hard as an oak and of long arms wrapping around her. In that moment, she felt cradled, cared for . . . Then she told herself that she was being ridiculous—he still had to get her down the ladder.

Her heart pounded in her ears as she frantically clutched his damp neck and opened her eyes. He was making low, soothing sounds from the back of his throat, whether for her or for himself, she didn't know, but somehow he was inching down the ladder. And then there were many hands to help and she was lifted from his arms and she knew a sudden and strange feeling of loss—almost as if she missed her rescuer in that moment. She felt her eyes well with tears and told herself it was because of the smoke.

She saw the circling red lights of an ambulance and started to struggle when she was placed on a gurney. She sat up abruptly.

"Wait! I can't go. I don't have any way to pay."

The ambulance attendant pushed her back down, and she started to struggle in earnest.

"Hey, Charley. Give me a second with her, okay?"

Ella looked up to see her rescuer from the ladder standing there. She knew it was he—she recognized his voice.

"Help me!" she sobbed, pleading at the thought of incurring a debt she could never manage.

"It's all right," he soothed.

She watched him lower the red handkerchief from over his mouth and nose; then he slipped off his hat and let it dangle behind his head.

She vaguely registered that he was good-looking, then savagely suppressed the thought. *Good looks have never done me any favors before . . .*

"Hey, what's your name?" he asked.

"Ella," she said after a long moment of thought. In some peculiar way, she both wanted to tell him everything about her life and wanted to let him know nothing.

"Ella. I'm Stephen, and you're shivering. Let them run you to the hospital to have a quick go-over. I'll tell you what . . . I'll pay for it, all right?"

She crossed her arms over her breasts. *I am shivering . . .* "What do you want me to do in exchange?" She lifted her chin and stared up into his eyes. *It's better to know . . .*

* * *

Stephen felt like someone had gut punched him—he understood the girl's question but was unprepared for it somehow. *What do I want?* His eyes took in her long, graceful neck and fine-boned shoulders. She looked like a half-starved kitten that still had some fight in her. His mind fused with the memory of the girls' laughter back at the station and he wondered vaguely what it would be like to flirt with this girl in front of him. *I am losing my mind . . .* He roughly grabbed a blanket from Charley and wrapped it around her shoulders. Her lips moved in thanks, but her teeth were chattering so badly she could barely speak.

"Delayed shock," he snapped. "I don't want anything in exchange, Ella. Just do what I ask for your own sake, okay?"

She lay down with visible reluctance, and he took her slender hand in his while Charley secured a belt across her hips.

"Ev—everything I have in the world is gone," she rambled, staring up at him.

"Don't worry," he muttered, feeling disgusted with himself for having more than a passing interest in her. He let go of her hand and turned away when Charley and his partner pushed the gurney into the ambulance. Stephen decided that once the scene was under control, he'd take a walk over to the hospital and see how she was doing and settle her bill. He told himself that he was simply being a gentleman and nothing else.

"I want the girl dead, and if you cannot accomplish the task, then I shall pay someone more competent." Douglas Nichols's whispery voice hissed through the phone line, and

Mitch Wagner once again felt a shiver of apprehension run down his spine. But he answered boldly just the same.

"I'm telling you I got it . . . You want the job done right, don't you? Nothing to tie it back to you . . ."

"Just finish what I paid you for . . . Oh, and my wife wants a word."

Mitch shifted his weight from one foot to the other. If Nichols was bad, his wife was a pit viper . . .

"Mitchell? Darling . . . what dear Douglas won't say is that if you do not get rid of that redheaded brat, you may find yourself—um—in the rather difficult situation of the hunter becoming the hunted . . . Do you take my meaning?"

"Yeah . . . I mean, yes. Yes, ma'am."

"Good, I'm so glad we've made that clear. Goodbye, darling."

Mitch slowly unwound the springy metal coil and put the receiver back on the hook. He left what had to be the only phone booth within fifty miles and decided to find the local diner, where he could get something to eat.

The image of his target's red hair hanging over the fireman's shoulder had been enough to make him want to choke. It was the second time she had evaded his grasp, and he was beginning to consider more dire and direct methods.

Chapter Two

Ella wet her lips when the young doctor asked her when her last menstrual cycle was—she knew exactly but had no idea what bearing the question had on her safety after the fire.

"What does it matter?" she asked coolly.

The doctor stared at her for a long moment. "How far along are you?" His gaze dropped to her belly and she automatically put a hand over the spot, pressing the voluminous hospital gown to her.

She set her jaw and met his blue eyes. "About five months." She knew that she barely showed because she was thin and so hungry half the time.

"Well," the doctor began, standing up, "your breathing seems good and you haven't been burned. Do you want me to examine you for the pregnancy?"

She shook her head quickly. "No . . . thank you."

"Do you have someplace to stay tonight? I imagine you lost pretty much everything in the fire."

"I'll be fine," she hastened to assure him.

He nodded. "Good enough, then."

He left her to put on her sooty blue and white dress,

and she tried to concentrate on the simple task, not daring to think beyond the moment.

Stephen paced the small waiting room and looked up when the doctor came out.

"So . . . my best friend is a hero, rescuing damsels in distress," the young physician teased.

"*Ach*, Nick . . . *kumme* on . . ." Stephen rubbed the back of his neck. "How is she?"

"Proud, poor, and pregnant."

For the second time that night, Stephen felt as if someone had punched him in the stomach—hard enough to drive the wind from his lungs.

"She's pregnant?" Stephen asked, looking for clarity and not knowing why it mattered so much to him that she was married.

"Keep it down, Steve . . . I'm not supposed to share that information with you."

"Where's the husband? Was he in the fire? Is he here?"

"I don't know." Nick shook his head, staring at him. "Why does it matter?"

Stephen glared at his friend. "I don't—it doesn't matter, I guess. Can I see her?"

"Sure. She'll be out in a few minutes."

Stephen nodded and watched Nick go back through the swinging doors.

The two men had become good friends that spring and shared a suite of rooms in a boardinghouse uptown when Stephen wasn't at the firehouse for his rotation. Stephen thought of the warm, well-appointed place he lived part of the time and wondered what it must have been like for Ella and her . . . husband to be living in that run-down firetrap of a building.

He looked up as the doors opened and Ella walked out. She didn't look much better than she had on the gurney, but something about her drew him in—made him want to touch her and . . . *I am completely* narrish, he told himself. *The girl's pregnant. . . .*

"Hello," he said, when she seemed about to walk right past him.

She startled, then looked up at him. "Uh—hello. Thank you again for tonight and what you did."

Stephen thought she sounded bleak, almost as though she didn't really think he'd done her any favors by getting her out of the fire.

He put a gentle hand on her thin left arm. "Hey—is your husband all right?"

Now he'd really gotten her attention, and her brown eyes widened. "Husband? I've never been married. Please excuse me."

He processed three things at once: that she was pregnant, not married, and obviously wanted to get away from him. "Sure—uh—Ella, but if you ever need anything, just stop by the fire station and ask for me—it's Stephen, okay?"

She nodded and he knew he'd already been dismissed from her mind.

Ella crept from the shelter of warmth and safety the hospital provided and went back out into the night. She heard the church bells ring and realized that it was four in the morning. *Not too long . . .*

. . . until daylight . . . She was suddenly catapulted back in time to one of her earliest memories—her father playing his violin, "playing to welcome the dawn," as he called it. Ella remembered standing in her warm white

nightgown and watching his capable fingers move over the finely stretched strings. It seemed as though her father's music did indeed usher in the dawn as the notes swelled and pinkness spread across the seascape sky. He played until the sun rose, and then he stopped to hug her close. It had felt as though nothing could ever come between them. But just seven years later death had stolen him from her. As a minor, she had been left in the care of an uncle and step-aunt she barely knew. One of the first things they'd done was to sell her father's beloved violin to "pay for her keep" in the grand house where she'd grown up.

Ella shook away the memories and concentrated instead on the sidewalk and the pattern of her steps. She knew where she had to go now and she wondered if she could stop what was to come—for the baby's sake. *For the baby's sake* . . . The words chased each other like synchronized swimmers around in her head until she felt a familiar rush of nausea. She stopped for a moment, found a wrinkled handkerchief in the pocket of her dress, and pressed it to her lips until the momentary queasiness passed.

She lifted her head and walked on, past the rows of nice homes and then the shops, and then over the railroad tracks, where she could still sense the acrid smell of smoke in the air. Her eyes traced the gaping spot in the landscape, like a gum with a lost tooth, and she sighed. Her room had been paid up at the boardinghouse for the following week—paid with the last of the money she'd managed to save—so now she had no choice . . .

Briefly, the firefighter's words drifted through her mind . . . *If you need anything* . . . His blue-green eyes had been earnest, but she knew she was being ridiculous to recall his words. Strangers, especially men, no matter how perfect they might seem, usually only wanted one thing from a girl. She rubbed absently at her belly, then pushed the thought aside. What Stephen the Firefighter did or did not want was of no concern to her . . .

Stephen sought his bed at the fire station but couldn't fall asleep. He was always keyed up after a fire, but tonight, he was positively restless, and he couldn't drag his thoughts from Ella. He turned her name over on his tongue, liking its simple syllables . . . *She's pregnant . . . Who'd leave a girl as brave as that red-haired scrapper to be pregnant and on her own? . . . But perhaps she chose it; wanted a baby to be part of her world so she wouldn't feel alone . . .* He jerked his thoughts up sharply, telling himself that he was a fool for trying to imagine what in the world went through a woman's mind, especially a pregnant woman who'd only jumped into his arms to escape certain death from the fire and chaos. He finally fell into a fitful sleep, somewhere on the edge of consciousness, and he was happy when he started to dream . . .

She was in his arms again, and her red hair hung loose, tendrils trailing over his shoulders and chest. He could feel the heat, both inside and out, and his mouth burned for want of tasting her lips. She leaned forward and he arched his back, trying to reach her—but she dissolved into a gray cloud of smoke, and he thought he heard a baby cry . . .

"You awake, Steve?"

It was Mike, the chief, and Stephen eased up on one elbow, glad to be free from the tantalizing dream. "Sure, what's going on?"

"Looks like that fire at the boardinghouse was no accident. Joey found two kerosene cans at the back of what was left of the place; they were empty and there was a fuse line."

"Who'd want to burn down a place where there were women . . . and babies?"

Stephen heard Mike sigh. "People can be sick in the soul, I guess . . . But, hey, I wanted to tell you something . . . I'm getting married."

"What?" Stephen scrambled to try to catch up with the conversation.

"Yeah—I know. Me."

"Is she—was she here last night?"

"Oh, you mean the girls from Millie's place—no, that was just a little last-minute fun."

Stephen thought he wasn't a prude, but even his sensibilities were shaken by the casual admission.

"Anyway, Steve—I want you to be a groomsman."

"A what?"

"You know, wear a suit, be part of the wedding party . . . Don't Amish have stuff like that?"

"Yeah, I guess so. Attendants and such."

"So, will you do it?"

Stephen nodded in the dimly lit room. "Sure. I'd be honored."

"Great. The wedding's two weeks away, so you can help plan the bachelor party. I was hoping we'd go to Millie's—just to look. No touching for me."

Stephen blinked. Millie's was a well-known house of ill repute that the men in town genially turned a blind eye to while the uptown ladies fumed. It was a well-run establishment by all accounts, though Stephen had done nothing more than look at the turret rooms from the outside of the place. He'd told himself he was interested in the architecture and subdued paint scheme, but to have a

Mike kind of party on the inside? It was enough to make an honest man nervous . . .

Once Mike left, Stephen felt less like sleeping than ever. Finally he gave up and headed out to the kitchen to have some coffee before the sun came up.

Ella stood on the steps of Millie's Social Club and stared long and hard at the dark paint on the ornate front door. Millie had told her she'd come crawling back, and here she was—fulfilling that sneering prediction. But, she knew it was warm and relatively safe inside, and despite Millie's snide comments, Ella knew that the older woman could have a soft heart now and then.

Ella drew a deep breath and held it before she knocked on the door . . . *I'll be a good mother . . . I will . . . I have to . . .*

Chapter Three

Mitch Wagner took a long pull on his cigarette and rubbed at the ache in the back of his neck. The hotel where he'd found a room was cheap and didn't provide much in the way of comfort, but it suited him fine, given the scant amount of money in his wallet. He'd nearly run through what Douglas Nichols had given him to do the job. He wasn't used to having much money in his possession, and the temptation to spoil himself a little had run far and fast.

He sighed, feeling lonely somehow. It was the town, he supposed—made him think of his boyhood and the pleasantness of his grandmother's house—it had always been an escape from his father's violence. He pushed such thoughts away and got resolutely to his feet. He crushed out the cigarette and went to the sink in the small bathroom. He splashed some water on his face and took a look in the mirror. Dark eyes peered back at him, sunken and cold, but he didn't waste too much time in reflection and instead went to get dressed to find out what he could about his elusive quarry.

* * *

"*Danki*, Abe." Stephen reached up and handed the envelope to the young Amish *buwe* sitting in the driver's seat of the old wagon. Stephen had made it a practice since he'd joined the fire company to send back part of his pay to Ice Mountain, to help support his *mamm* and *aenti*. Stephen knew that his mother would far prefer that he bring the money himself, but he had no desire to go back often to the small Amish community where he was raised—where he had once been called a murderer by even his own family . . .

He sighed to himself as he watched Abe drive away. Nee*, going back to Ice Mountain will probably never appeal to me . . .*

"Hey there, watch it!" The brusque voice of a passerby reminded him that he was standing in the middle of the brick sidewalk. He moved to one side, then started his errands for the morning.

He was on at the firehouse five days, then off for two, and though he might have stayed at the station even then, he liked living the odd day with Nick . . . *Especially when he can help the people I rescue . . .* He pushed the thought away, only to realize that he was discreetly eyeing the passersby, looking for a bright red head of hair. *Ella . . .*

"Whoa there, young Stephen. Where is your mind this fine morning?"

Stephen looked down into the watery blue eyes of the *auld* man who regularly inhabited a chair outside the general store. Lester Pike was blind, but he seemed to have a sight beyond the vision of most people and had no trouble identifying various folks in town or winning at board games.

"I guess my mind is wandering," Stephen admitted with a smile.

"You know, I have the cure for that," Lester said jovially.

"Checkers?"

"Checkers! Have a seat and tell me about the fire last night."

Stephen dropped into the chair opposite his friend and shrugged his shoulders. "Not much to tell, really."

"Heard you rescued a girl."

"*Nee*, she—I didn't—"

"Come on, boy. Heard she's a pretty redhead who works down at Millie's."

Stephen dropped a checker. "What? She—where?"

"King me. Sure, you know I've been friends with Millie longer than that dear woman would care to admit—"

"Lester. Wait. Are you sure about El—I mean, the girl from the fire?"

"Hmm? Oh my, yes. Of course, you being Amish, ya probably wouldn't pay much mind to a place like Millie's, but—"

Stephen got to his feet. "Lester, I'm sorry, but I've got to go and check on something. I'll stop back later and finish our game."

"You were losing anyway."

"Tell me about it," Stephen muttered, then hurried off down the street.

Mitch squinted in the bright morning light and headed for the diner. The babble of the townspeople was irritating, and he felt even more frustrated when someone reached out and touched his hand. He paused, then drew away sharply when he looked down into a blind man's eyes.

"Here, pop—here's a dollar. I don't have time to hear your sob story." Mitch threw a dollar from his wallet onto the checkerboard, and the blind man laughed out loud.

"Son, I thank you, but I'm not begging; I'm playing checkers."

"Yeah, well, whatever." Mitch had started to move again when the blind man called to him.

"You're new in town, aren't you?"

Mitch turned on his heel and went back to the checkerboard. "How do you know?" he asked suspiciously.

"I just know . . . My name's Lester Pike, and I know everything there is to know about everybody hereabouts."

Mitch considered. *Maybe the old dog can give me some leads on my target . . .*

"Hey there, pop, I'll tell you what—how 'bout we use that dollar and I'll buy you a late breakfast?"

The blind man smiled and held out his hand. "I'd be glad to, Mitch."

Mitch had a sudden uneasy feeling, as if someone had shined a light on his insides for a moment. "Hey, how'd you know my name? I never told you."

"Oh, just a right guess, then. Let's go to the diner and I'll tell you all the local news."

Lester Pike got to his feet and laid a hand once more on Mitch's arm.

Mitch realized that he had never felt the gentle touch of an older man—his father had been—

"Let's get a move on, son, before Betty turns the menu over to lunch at the diner."

"R—right." Mitch fumbled in his mind, somehow

wondering if spending time with the blind man had actually been his idea after all.

He walked through the passersby with Lester Pike's hand still on his arm, and he felt himself shiver as they entered the bustling café.

A smiling waitress with a white cap and a blue dress indicated an open booth. "Have a seat, fellas. Lester, who's your friend?"

"Oh, forgive me, Betty—this is Mitch. He's new in town."

Mitch gave the woman an abrupt nod and slid into the booth opposite the blind man.

"Coffee for both of you?"

Mitch nodded while Lester gave a genial reply.

Betty turned to go to the counter and Mitch drummed his thin fingers against the tabletop nervously.

"Take it easy, son. You sure must be hungry, and in more ways than one."

Mitch stared into the other man's seemingly sightless eyes. "Whadda ya mean, pop? More ways than one? Why ya gotta say things like that?"

"I suppose it's an old way of speaking—I just thought maybe your heart and mind might be hungry too."

Mitch suddenly wanted to flee the booth, but the smiling Betty was back with the coffee. "Now, what'll you boys have?" she asked pleasantly.

Mitch swallowed. "Bacon and eggs—scrambled."

"And the usual, Lester?"

"Yep—by the way, how's your mother feeling after her fall?"

Betty lit up like a Christmas bulb as she bubbled a response, much to Mitch's discomfiture. The blind guy sure had a way with people—and maybe he knew Ella Nichols just as well. The thought kept Mitch in his seat.

"Did you finish high school, Mitch?" Lester asked as he sipped at his hot coffee.

"What?"

"High school? Did you make it all the way through?"

Mitch thought back to his senior year and all the days and nights he'd spent nursing the drunk of a father who'd abused him. He never could understand why he did it . . . why he cared for the bastard . . . but it had cost him graduating and sent him adrift into the world.

Mitch drew a deep breath and refocused, remembering he was sitting in a diner and his breakfast had been set before him. He picked up a fork with a hand that shook slightly.

"Why don't I ask some questions, pop?" he drawled, trying to find his footing in the casualness of his tone.

"Of course. What do you want to know?"

"Well . . . see, like ya said, I'm new in town. Anybody else new? Maybe a woman, like . . . It would be nice to meet a girl, ya know?"

Lester smiled. "You know, Mitch, I truly believe that you mean that . . . It would be nice for you to have a loving wife."

"Whoa!" Mitch pointed with his fork. "I ain't sayin' wife."

"Aren't you? I must have misunderstood."

But Mitch doubted there was any misunderstanding. He himself was beginning to understand that the blind man knew exactly what was true, and the realization shook Mitch through to a place deep beneath his cold heart . . .

* * *

Ella balanced the silver tray in two hands and tried not to look down at the coddled eggs that wiggled on the plate. Miss Millie ate well, Ella considered. *But not anything that I would enjoy having . . .* Which, of course, reminded her of her empty stomach. She had to swallow hard before stretching to knock on the heavy oaken door.

"Come in!" Millie called.

Ella wet her lips, steeling herself against the coming questions, then opened the door. She clung to the ornate knob for a moment, letting the circular pattern in the metal soothe her as she met Millie's gaze. She'd saved all her money for weeks, hoping to find a way to leave Millie's behind her. She'd finally managed to move to the boardinghouse, a step up from living in a house of ill repute. But now here she was again, back where she'd started.

"Where's Sasha?" The question was brusque. *But at least she's not tossing me out . . . yet . . .*

"I told her to go back to sleep . . . she woke to let me in this morning."

"You told her? And exactly who are you, miss, to give orders in my house?"

Here we go . . . Please, if you hear me, God, let her be merciful . . . Ella advanced toward the high four-poster walnut bed and stared into the green eyes and the aged, though still pretty, face of the woman who was the soul of the house.

"I'm no one to give orders, Miss Millie—I just thought that—"

"Bring the tray here and stop thinking—it's what softens a woman—and you are going to have to be harder than nails when that babe arrives. This town might look pretty on the outside, but the wind blows cold enough once judgment gets hold of some folks hereabouts."

Ella nodded and settled the tray on the ample lap of the older woman. She stepped back and waited, still trying to ignore the eggs.

Millie flung her hennaed hair over her shoulder and lifted a fork. She arched a penciled brow as she tasted her eggs and eyed Ella with seeming dispassion. "There's soot on your dress."

"I was in the fire last night—at the boardinghouse."

"So I heard. Quite a show, that fire. And yet, you survived."

Ella felt herself flush a bit at the sudden remembrance of the fireman's arms around her. "Yes . . . the fire crew was very helpful."

"I can imagine," Millie returned drily. "But no matter. Though I might tell you that there was talk here last night. Some of the girls heard that fire might have been more than it seemed to be."

A sudden dread filled Ella's chest. "Wh—what do you mean?"

Millie applied herself to her toast with hearty bites. "Arson. And you know—they say that arson is mixed up with violence and sex in the twisted mind."

"I—I didn't know—I . . ." Ella stammered, her thoughts racing.

"Well, knowing what I do about your background"—Millie pointed at her with the edge of a buttered crust—"I have a hunch that somebody wants you dead, little girl. Now, what do you think of that?"

Ella's reply was to promptly throw up on the Aubusson carpet, much to Millie's displeasure.

* * *

"Why didn't you tell me?"

Stephen followed Nick down the hall of the hospital, trying to keep his voice down.

"You think I make it a habit to visit Millie's beyond seeing to the medical care of the girls?"

"You see to their medical care?" Stephen felt surprise at the admission. "You mean, you've had to perform an—"

"Perform an abortion? No, my friend I haven't, and I wouldn't unless the mother's life was in grave peril. But besides that, women have other medical needs. You do know that, right?"

Stephen frowned at his friend; then another thought struck him. "Have you—taken care of Ella?"

"Beyond last night, I've never seen her before. Look, I've got rounds. If you are so struck by her, why not go down to Millie's and ask for her?"

Stephen's mind boggled at the suggestion, and Nick must have seen the look on his face. "Ask to *talk* to her, all right? You straitlaced Amish man."

Ella was more than relieved to slip between crisp linen sheets and lay her head on the goose down pillow, glad of a few minutes' rest. She'd managed to secure her old position at Millie's establishment and was grateful, even though it would mean a lot of hard work and would become increasingly difficult with her advancing pregnancy. She rolled from her side to her back and stared up at the overhead crystal chandelier—almost, she could look at the elaborate light fixture and imagine herself home by the sea. But that made her think of Jeremy, and thinking of Jeremy made her cry.

She blew out a breath of frustration and swiped at her eyes. *I was so foolish—I should have known that someone like Jeremy was too good to be true.* His looks, temperament, and seemingly earnest expressions of love had all been a façade to lure her in, and she had taken the bait like a starving trout. She'd given herself to him body and soul, on one single occasion. When she'd discovered she was pregnant, she'd expected he might be surprised, but had never imagined his brutal dismissal of her. He'd been furious, and she had known fear when he grabbed her, shaking her so hard that her teeth rattled.

She could still hear his voice, savage and ruthless. "Get rid of it! Do you understand, you stupid fool? Get rid of it any way you can."

Instead, she had fled the small seaside town, leaving behind all she knew. But misfortune seemed to have followed her, like the fire in the boardinghouse, and she sometimes had the strange feeling that she was being watched. She wondered if someone from her old life could truly want her dead . . . Once she'd fled Jeremy, she'd ridden the railroad deep into Pennsylvania and had finally ended up in Coudersport—weak and broken—both in pocket and in spirit. She'd gone to Millie's unwittingly, not knowing what sort of house it was, but there she had finally found work that would allow her to live. Now that the money she'd saved was gone, she would have to remain here until after her baby was born. She couldn't risk another move at this late date.

She turned once more in the bed, trying to get comfortable, then heard the large clock downstairs toll ten a.m. She sat up and decided she'd better start her day . . .

Chapter Four

Stephen paced the back streets of town, having absolutely no idea what he'd say to Ella even if he did get a chance to talk with her. But he rationalized that he had to make arrangements for Mike's party, so it wouldn't hurt to go to Millie's. With this in mind, he finally turned in the direction of the big *haus*. He got there, then blew out a harsh breath before he mounted the steps and pushed the ornate bell. He heard the echo of the sound from somewhere deep within; then the heavy wooden door was eased open wide.

"We ain't open for business yet," the petite, dark-haired girl said. "But," she added, a smile warming her eyes, "we might always make an exception for someone who looks like you."

Stephen shook his head with a smile, trying to ignore her revealing gown. "I'm looking for a pregnant girl."

She frowned, then flounced backward. An older female voice called from within. "Let the gentleman enter, Sasha."

The girl allowed him to pass with a petulant look. He felt his boots slip into thick burgundy carpeting, and a brief glance around told him that only the finest of woods decorated the interior of the room.

He felt vaguely like he was entering the domain of a queen as he approached the older woman who sat poised and confident on a velvet settee on the far side of the room.

"Miss Millie?"

"Yes, honey . . . It's your first time here, right?" she asked smoothly.

He nodded briefly, then repeated himself. "Look, I—does a pregnant girl work here?"

The older woman's painted eyebrows inched up a fraction. "We don't do none of that strange stuff here, honey. You'll have to settle for the regular menu . . ." She pointed to a carefully lettered sign that hung on the wall in an ornate frame.

Stephen lifted his gaze and blinked. He felt his face grow red at the blatant descriptions and prices listed.

"*Nee*—no, I mean, I just wanted to talk—"

He broke off when a broom clattered noisily down the curved staircase that took up much of the hall to his left. Hurried footsteps followed the bristles, and Stephen felt his heartbeat begin to pick up. He thought he was seeing things for a moment, but then he half shook his head and realized that there was no mistaking the long red hair. It was Ella, the girl he'd saved from the flames and who'd visited his dream the night before.

She stared at him, her red lips forming an "O" of surprise, and then she scurried away up the stairs. He wanted to throw down the money in his wallet and *geh* after her. He wanted to beg to let her be with him in a room for an hour—just to talk. *Yeah, right,* his mind mocked. *You've been wanting to kiss her since the fire . . .*

He ruthlessly tamped down his desire and had turned

to speak to Miss Millie when another girl entered the room and glided across the carpet to him. He felt the press of the petite female body against his front and looked down into sparkling blue eyes and pink, smiling lips. The girl reached up and gently looped her arms about his shoulders, then pressed even closer. He could feel her soft body against his chest but knew no arousal—*Because I'm stuck on Ella . . . Red-haired Ella . . . Ella who works here . . .*

He glanced at Miss Millie, who was watching him with a disconcerting appraisal in her eyes. "Come now, Anna. I don't think the gentleman prefers blondes."

The girl in his arms pouted, then pressed a quick kiss against his cheek before backing away.

"So it's our Ella who you want?" Miss Millie asked, and he knew he was flushed with his answer.

"Yes, but just to—"

Millie held up an imperious white hand. "I know—just to talk."

He thought he heard the girl called Sasha give a faint protest, but Miss Millie shook her head in dismissal to the girl.

"Very well. Go on up after her, honey. I believe she's in the front bedroom." There was something enigmatic in Miss Millie's words, but he didn't want to take time to think about it. He glanced once more at the flagrant, hanging menu, then felt for his wallet—wishing that "talking" was listed somewhere.

"No charge for the first time, honey."

"Uh . . . oh," he muttered. "*Danki.*"

He'd slipped into the dialect of the Amish but didn't care as his hand met the smooth balustrade and he began to climb the polished staircase with quick steps . . .

* * *

Ella forced herself to focus on pouring lemon oil into a clean cloth and tried not to think about the fireman she'd seen downstairs . . . but it was no use. She would have been lying to herself if she said that she didn't think him attractive. She found that the image of his face and form burned behind her eyes. And even more powerfully, her artistic nature recognized that he was truly beautiful, someone she'd love to paint. His dark hair was cropped close to his head and his blue-green eyes were lined with thick lashes that brushed his flushed cheeks. His shoulders were broad and his waist trim and his hands . . . Oh, she shivered at the thought of his large, lean-fingered, competent-looking hands. *Hands that held me, cradled me . . .*

After Jeremy's quick actions, she understood the mechanics of sex—but there was something more involved with the firefighter—something tantalizing and bracing, both at the same time—like the salt spray and wind of the ocean at dawn. *And you're pregnant, my fine miss . . . by another hatefully good-looking man . . .*

She started when there was a slow knock on the door. By some strange intuition, she knew it was he—Stephen—and she felt an odd tingling. "Come in," she called, forcing her voice to sound hard. *Remember what happened with Jeremy . . . Remember . . .*

The door was eased open and he entered. She gave him a brisk nod, then set about focusing on dusting the bedside table. She lifted a small marble hippo from the wood, then put it back down again when he didn't speak.

She straightened her back and turned to face him, glad of the expanse the big white coverlet-strewn bed between them provided. "What is it?" she asked.

"I wanted to talk . . . that's all."

She clutched her dusting cloth tightly. "I thanked you already for saving me. You said you wanted nothing for

paying my hospital fee. Have you changed your mind?"
Because I'm not for sale . . . Not, not, not . . .

"*Nee, sei se gut*—I mean, no, I haven't."

"Why," she exclaimed, studying him more carefully, "you're Amish . . ."

Stephen swallowed and nodded. "Yeah, but I guess I don't spread that around so much."

"Where is your Amish community?"

"You—you know about the Amish?"

She smiled faintly, and he felt like warmed syrup was running down his spine at the endearing glimpse of her pearl white teeth. "When I was—when I was traveling here, the train had a stopover for a few hours at a town called Renew. I was sort of hungry, and a kind Amish woman had a small stand at the depot. She seemed to know that I didn't have much money, and she gave me a cheese sandwich and a ripe red tomato to eat. She wouldn't take any coins and—" Ella shrugged. "She talked to me a lot—some in English and some like you just did. I— I've never forgotten."

She looked back to the cleaning rag she held, seemingly embarrassed by her torrent of speech, and he wanted to *geh* round the bed and touch her, comfort her. But he stood still and cleared his throat. "I come from a place called Ice Mountain—you might have heard of it. Anyway, that's where I lived until—until I came here and started work at the station."

"Why did you leave?"

It was an innocent question and softly spoken, but it roused an assault of memories in his mind—his *mamm*'s sobbing accusations and his *aenti*'s chilling glare, the feel of the worn shovel handle as he dug the grave . . . He came back to himself abruptly and saw Ella waiting for his response. "It no longer felt like home," he said. "Why did you come here?"

He realized how personal the question was, given their surroundings, and regretted it deeply when she pressed a hand against her belly, smoothing down the simple house-dress she wore. But then she smiled again and raised her chin. "The place I was raised—it no longer felt like home."

They laughed together softly at her joke, and he had the strange feeling that he'd known her for a long time and had only been waiting for her to come into his life. *I'm narrish,* he told himself. *Crazy as can be . . .*

But being crazy didn't stop him from taking a few steps around the bottom of the large bed. He noticed her tense up and he stood still. "I just want to talk," he soothed. "Nothing from the—uh, menu."

He saw the puzzled look on her face, and then she gasped and put a hand to her mouth, giggling. He squared his shoulders, wondering what he'd done to seem so fool-ish when she drew her fingers from her lips and shook her head. "I'm so sorry. You thought that I work here?"

He exhaled roughly. "Well, don't you?"

"Oh, yes, I do." Her beautiful smile was wide. "But I'm the housekeeper."

Chapter Five

Ella still smiled as she dusted—the look of consternation on the fireman's handsome face had quickly been accompanied by a ruddy flush as he'd stumbled to apologize. She'd come round the bed and held out her hand, not wanting him to feel so embarrassed. "Please," she'd said shyly. "Can we be friends?" It was an odd, impulsive request, like jumping into the surf of the Atlantic in the gloaming and expecting the water to be warm . . .

But he'd taken her hand readily in a firm handshake, and she'd felt as though some electric current had simmered through her fingers at his brief touch. *Funny, I never felt such a thing with Jeremy . . .* Then Stephen had backed away with a nod. "*Jah*, friends." His tone had been brisk but warm, and she'd watched him walk out of the room, wondering if he'd truly meant the friendship that he'd pledged . . .

"The housekeeper?" Nick repeated, and Stephen let his head loll back as he sat in a comfortable chair in their rooms. It was evening, and Stephen had not found much peace on his off day.

"I know," he muttered. "I know. I looked like a damn ass, and I suppose I was a laughingstock to that Miss Millie and her girls."

Nick chuckled. "Aw, Miss Millie meant no harm. But I would have given anything to have seen your face . . . And you an Amish man, at that."

Stephen lifted his head to give his friend a sour smile. "She asked about me being Amisch—Ella did. I'd let some Penn Dutch slip and she recognized it."

Nick sobered instantly. "I'm sorry. I know it's hard for you to talk about Ice Mountain, but . . ." His friend paused. "It's also not good for your health to hold bitterness inside for long."

"Is that the doctor talking or my friend?"

"Both."

Stephen gave him a rueful smile. "Part and parcel of telling you the truth, I suppose."

"You were proven innocent of the false accusations against you." Nick put his glass on a nearby table and leaned forward in his chair. "Innocent . . ."

"Yeah, but I didn't feel innocent. They all shunned me, except Joel."

"The one who is now their spiritual leader? What do you think *he'd* want you to feel?"

"Joel is—different somehow from the others. Look, Nick, I know you're trying to help, but I just need to clear my head. I think I'll go for a walk."

Nick sighed. "All right, but how about not walking down to Millie's Social Club?"

Stephen punched his friend's shoulder lightly, then set out in the early evening. People were scarce on the brick

sidewalks. *Everybody's probably home having supper . . .*
He was about to go into Davidson's Pharmacy to get a
birch beer when a faint sound made him pause. He turned
his head and listened hard. The splash of water came to
him and he immediately began to move in the direction of
the town's large pond. The place was good for fishing but
lacked a safe fence, and the water was especially deep and
murky.

His steps quickened, and then he was running full-out
when he heard a scream and a garbled cry for help . . .

Mitch thought back to the kindness of Lester Pike and
tried to turn it over in his mind. Lester had told him
straight that a fairly new-to-town redhead worked as a
housekeeper in the local bawdy house, and it had taken
very little for Mitch to bide his time, then hide beneath
one of Millie's downstairs open windows in the dimness
of the evening. He knew women chattered like jays, and
it wasn't long before someone told a girl called Ella that
she was to run to the drugstore for some bicarbonate.

Mitch followed Ella with soft footsteps; the telltale red
hair made him sure of his prize. He couldn't believe his
luck in getting her alone in the dark. He fingered the edge
of the knife he carried, almost ready to make his move.
Then Ella flicked on a flashlight, and Mitch fell to his
knees at the unexpected brilliance of the light. It seemed
like noon, and he dropped the knife. He was suddenly
unable to move and could only fix his gaze on the wash
of light in front of him. He swiped at his face, thinking
he'd had too much to drink, but the light persisted. And
then, in his mind's eye, he saw himself having breakfast
with the blind man. What had he said? Something about

changing direction and God's love chasing him . . . Mitch
shook his head and slowly came back to himself as he
heard the splashing of the pond water. He bent down and
fumbled for the knife in the sudden darkness. *Am I losing
my mind?* Mitch muttered a curse and stayed still as he
watched and listened . . .

Ella was admiring the lightning bugs as she walked the
road to downtown. For a moment, she could remember
being young and catching the beautiful things in her
hands, but never being willing to put them in a jar overnight. She hated to see anything trapped . . . She sighed
to herself and turned her flashlight on. She truly didn't
mind going to the pharmacy to run errands late for
Millie—it kept her from being in close contact with most
townsfolk. She valued her privacy and was still surprised
at herself for asking Stephen to be her friend. She didn't
have many friends in town, except maybe blind and
congenial Lester Pike . . .

She stopped abruptly when she heard a frantic splashing and turned the beam of her light into the cattails that
grew up around the town's pond. A faint cry for help
reached her ears, and then eerily nothing, and she knew
by instinct that someone was drowning. But Ella was a
strong swimmer, having learned in the sea, and she didn't
panic now.

She dropped her small purse on the ground and surged
forward into the edge of the pond. The ground was
mucky, and she lost her cheap pair of shoes within three
steps, but she plunged on, her flashlight in her hand. She
hoped the beam of light might show some ripple in the
pond's surface, if the victim had gone under already. But

the dark was closing in and she despaired of seeing anyone until the urgent sound of a dog barking from the opposite bank made her turn. She was about to kick off into the deeper water when an arm slid around her waist, holding her fast. She would have screamed, but then she recognized the voice that sounded close in her ear.

"Let me," Stephen ordered in his firefighter's tell-everyone-what to do voice. He tried to pull her behind him, but she shook him off. "I can outswim you any day," she breathed, then dove beneath the surface of the pond . . .

Stephen swam, following the now-frail beam of light as it sank into the water. His heart hammered fast and hard at the thought of Ella and the baby drowning. *Please, Gott—let her be all right and her baby and whoever else that You can see in this water . . .* One part of his brain prayed in repetition while another tried to peer through the mucky water. He sought to touch bottom and couldn't, then got to the surface to check his bearings. Ella came up not more than two feet in front of him.

"I've got him," she gasped.

Stephen reached to take the young boy from her arms. "Hold on to my shoulders!" he cried as he turned, but Ella was already swimming past him and soon stood in the weeds of the bank.

They sloshed to land together, and Stephen put the child down on dry ground.

By now, the barking dog must have alerted somebody from town, and Stephen saw the rapid approach of a lantern's light even as he turned the boy on his side and slapped his back hard.

Blind Lester Pike somehow had gotten to them, and by

the light of the swinging lantern the old man held, Stephen could see that the boy's skin was ominously blue.

"He's not breathin'," Lester said softly.

"He'll breathe," Stephen snapped, turning the boy back over and pushing on his stomach. Water and mucus spurted weakly from the child's blue lips, and Stephen felt sick inside. *Please,* Gott, *let this little one of yours live . . . Sei se gut . . . please . . .*

"Do somethin', girl." Lester's words seemed far away, and Stephen sank back on his heels and watched in amazement as Ella leaned over and covered the child's small mouth and nose with her own lips. She also tilted the little blue chin upward as she worked. Stephen gathered her long, wet hair in his hands and held it back so he could differentiate between the light and the shadows, watching her intently.

Lester cleared his throat and spoke with reverence. "'Tis only God Who gives the Breath of Life. We pray that He does so here . . ."

Suddenly there was the sound of a deep inhalation, and then retching, and lastly, the beautiful sound of the boy gagging and spitting up the water that had kept him from breathing. He choked, and Ella sat him up. Stephen saw that the previous blue of the child's skin was fading quickly into a pale but healthy color.

"He'll do now," Lester grunted. Then the sound of the barking dog grew louder, and a beagle rushed under the lantern to land on the little boy's lap, wiggling ecstatically.

Stephen heard Ella laugh with relief, and the sound filled him like a rushing creek. "You saved his life, Ella." He realized that he was still holding strands of her hair and quickly let go.

She stared at him in the mellow lantern light, and he swiped at his own hair, feeling water running down his cheek.

"We both did," she answered briefly.

"I—I'm glad somebody did," the boy said in weak tones.

Stephen looked up into Lester's blind eyes, and the old man smiled. "And praise be to God fer that."

Mitch stayed on his knees, his heart thumping at the sounds and scene being played out before him. He kept remembering the light and the way the girl had breathed life into the child, then told himself he was an idiot. He had a job to do, and all this God stuff was driving him crazy. . . .

But, deep in his mind, the words hummed over and over in a mocking refrain: *You ain't never killed before . . . You ain't never murdered more . . . Then why am I willing to do it now?* Something primal and savage rose up in him as he remembered all of the abuse he'd suffered. *I was dead a long time ago, murdered by my father. What difference does it make if I kill now? No one can punish a dead man anyways . . .*

Chapter Six

The next half hour followed in a whirlwind for Ella as the boy's parents finally came. Stephen introduced them to Ella as Mr. and Mrs. Toole. Ma Toole hugged the soaking boy tight, then shook the child as if she couldn't believe that he was real.

"I snuck out ta catch bullfrogs, Ma."

"That's all right then, Jackie," Pa Toole said in his mild way. "It just seems that the water must've come too close fer comfort."

Everyone laughed, and Ella and Stephen were both hugged with gratitude.

Lester Pike handed Stephen the lantern and ambled off in the darkness, and now Ella stood alone with Stephen, finally aware that she was soaking wet and that the smell of the pond clung to her.

"You've got to come home with me and dry off," Stephen insisted when she would have turned to go. "It's too long a walk back to Millie's for you and the baby— I mean—uh . . ."

Ella whirled and looked up at him. "The baby? How

do you know?" *And what do you think of me, O Stephen with eyes like the sea . . .*

He shrugged. "I just know."

"That means the whole town must know," Ella muttered. She reached down to scoop up her purse and had started to walk away when he caught her lightly by the arm.

"*Sei se gut*, Ella—Friends . . . Remember?"

She stopped and reluctantly turned around. "You still want to be friends, knowing that I"—she paused, then went on with determination—"I gave myself to a man with no wedding?"

"*Nee* mistake, Ella. The Amish believe that *Gott* is the Giver of life. You wouldn't have that life inside you unless it was meant to be. Again, *nee* mistake . . . and I don't care about what is past."

He took a step closer to her, and she wanted to melt into him, to feel him hold her close. *What am I thinking? He's simply being kind . . .* She shivered, and he spoke with clear determination. "That's it. I'm not going to let you and the ba—you—catch pneumonia standing out here."

She sighed to herself. *I am tired after the experience tonight . . . I guess it wouldn't hurt to go with him and—*

"Ella?"

"Yes," she said finally. "I'll go with you . . . my friend."

Pregnant? The word struck like ice to the bottom of Mitch's soul as he crouched in the bushes near the pond. Douglas Nichols and the Pit Viper must not know she was pregnant, or maybe they wouldn't have sent someone to get rid of her. In truth, Mitch knew little of the reasons behind their scheme—only that he'd been paid a great deal of money. Of course, he'd heard rumors in the seaside town that had something to do with a will and that fancy house, the Glass Castle . . . He felt a cramp in his leg that jolted him back to the present, and he almost stood up, but she was still there talking to the tall fireman. Mitch inched backward over the ground, trying to ease his leg. It was dark all around him, but in his head he kept seeing images of the strange light that emanated from the girl.

He decided he needed more sleep to get things right in his head and started to walk in the dark.

Her friend . . . her friend . . . that's what I pledged to be . . . Not some lusting man who would love to taste her mouth and—

Stephen snapped back to awareness as Ella came out of Nick's room, swathed in a burgundy-colored robe.

"Hiya." He smiled, glad that Nick wasn't there to see him standing around like some addlepated fool.

"Hi . . . So your roommate is the doctor . . . from the hospital?" She flushed slightly. "I saw all the science equipment in his room . . . He told you that I'm pregnant, didn't he?"

He reached to rub the back of his neck. "Well—he might have let it slip."

She nodded, and he drew a deep breath. He was infinitely glad that when they'd arrived at his rooms, he'd discovered a scrawled note from Nick saying that he was out on a difficult case and didn't expect to be back until late.

Stephen sought a safe topic of conversation as he indicated the chair near the fireplace. He sat down opposite her. *Talk about something other than pregnancy and sex . . .* He cleared his throat. "What you did with that *buwe* . . . how you put your mouth on his . . . I've never thought of that."

She shrugged. "I grew up by the sea and children sometimes get in too deep. Although I know that it's now called mouth-to-mouth ventilation. You're trying to breathe for the other person. It's simple, really."

"It was *wunderbaar* to watch and I like your description— breathing for the other . . . I guess that's what we're supposed to do sometimes . . ." He didn't stop to analyze why he allowed his Penn Dutch to slip in when he was with Ella; he only knew that he felt at peace for the first time in what seemed a very long time. He looked at her and found her dark eyes studying him.

"What is it?" he asked hoarsely.

"Have you ever wanted someone to do that for you— breathe for you, I mean?" She laughed in a wistful way. "I probably sound strange . . ."

"*Nee*," he whispered. "I know what you mean—someone to support you, believe in you, and help you through the rough patches so that you *kumme* out stronger—I suppose that's what love does."

He watched her turn to study the low flames and waited in the expectant silence, wondering if he'd spoken oddly or out of turn.

"Yes," she murmured after a moment. "Love should do that."

Unwillingly, his gaze slid to her stomach in the over-sized robe. *Somebody didn't love her—the father of her baby* . . . He checked his morose train of thought and was about to ask her about her life by the sea when there was a sharp knock at the door. "Excuse me," he said, knowing that Nick wouldn't knock, which could only mean one thing . . . His landlady, Dora Broom, had caught wind of a woman in his room. . . .

Ella blinked back the tears in her eyes. *How is it . . . that in this strange, mountainous place I have found someone who understands my heart, who understands love . . .* But the older woman at the door had a carrying voice, and Ella stiffened as she overheard the sharp words.

"'Ere now, Mr. Lambert—What have I told ya? You know I don't hold with havin' womenfolk up here, and it'll do no good to say she's one of the doctor's patients, neither . . . Besides, she ain't the kind for you—she works at Millie's Social Club." This last was said so loudly that Ella clutched her hands in her lap. *I'm not the kind for him . . . maybe she's right . . . What am I thinking? Just because he talks about love doesn't mean much—Jeremy talked about it too . . .*

But then Ella heard Stephen respond in even tones. "Just tonight Miss Nichols revived little Jackie Toole when he might have died from drowning in the pond."

Ella saw the woman's round face and boot black eyes as she peered around Stephen's straight back. "Ya don't say, Mr. Lambert? Well, ain't that something . . . I know what she needs—what y'uns both need—one of my keg cider hot toddies, that's what. I'll have the mister go down into the cellar to fetch a fresh batch. I'll be right back."

Ella smiled at the turn of conversation as she heard the woman trot off down the steps. Stephen closed the door with an audible sigh, then came back to where she sat.

"I'm sorry—don't mind Mrs. Broom. She's nosy but basically harmless."

"Well, as tempting as one of Mrs. Broom's toddies sounds, I think I'd better go. It'll be quite dark walking back to Millie's." She rose in the burgundy robe, but he put out a hand to hold her still for a moment.

"Don't," he whispered. "Please don't *geh*."

He watched her eyes darken and smiled faintly. "I mean, stay for the hot toddy, and I'll tell you a story about where I grew up."

She frowned a bit. "About the place you said no longer feels like home? Stephen, you don't have to."

He eased her back into her chair. "*Kumme*, let me sing for my supper, as it were . . ."

Ella lifted an eyebrow at him. "You mean, you're spinning a yarn for my company?"

"*Jah* . . . it is well worth it." His gaze held hers steadily, and she finally nodded.

He sat down opposite her and stretched out his legs. "Well, let's see—I got in trouble a lot as a *buwe*."

"You were rambunctious?" she teased softly.

"Something like that—but in any case, when I was in trouble at home, I used to visit this *auld* lady who lived in a cabin in the high timber. I called her Frau Birdy—she could imitate any bird sound on the mountain. It was remarkable—much more than mere whistling . . ."

His mind wandered briefly as he thought of the old woman, now long dead. He owed his life to her, he supposed. When he'd been sixteen, he'd caught a bad chest cold, much worse than he'd even realized at the time—but he hadn't been home in days and wasn't about to *geh* when he was ill and feeling vulnerable. He would have received little care or compassion from his *mamm* or *aenti*. And, running wild in the high timber, he'd been too sick to even make it to the healer, so Frau Birdy had taken him in and nursed him back to health.

"What are you thinking?" Ella asked. "You stopped your story."

He smiled at her and shook his head. "I guess I'm not so *gut* at spinning a yarn and I—"

A brisk knock on the door brought him to his feet, and he went to open it. Mrs. Broom passed him a laden tray, and he thanked her politely.

"Now you an' the girl drink these down straight—yours is on the left here, Mr. Lambert—the mister made it a bit stronger. They'll warm ya up right fast." Stephen saw the elderly woman shoot a now-appreciative glance at Ella and couldn't resist a smile as he closed the door.

He carried the tray to a small round table in front of Ella and handed her the steaming mug on his right. He sat down and lifted his own concoction, watching her take her first sip. She shivered as she swallowed. "Oh my." She smiled. "This is good."

He took a sip of his own and couldn't suppress a cough. It tasted like some burning combination of many forms of alcohol, but watching her run the tip of her tongue over her lips, he wasn't sure which was more intoxicating—the drink or simply Ella herself. The thought warmed him, and as he drank, he began to answer her questions about Ice Mountain more easily.

"So, do you have many brothers and sisters?"

"*Nee.* I know the proverbial joke is that Amish families have seventeen children or more, but I'm an only child."

He watched her place a hand over her belly in an absent fashion as she nodded. "So am I."

"Then we have that in common, but as for the babe you carry, I'll tell you an Amish blessing: May your lap be full of *kinner.*"

"Full of children?" she guessed.

"*Jah* . . . it would be good to have a brother or sister to talk things over with in life." He knew he sounded faintly wistful but realized that he'd derailed the conversation when she put her glass down quickly.

"I think I'll need to manage this baby first . . . and I should go."

He drained his mug and told himself he'd been stupid to burden her with thoughts of other children.

"I'll take you back."

"I—I'm sorry—I wasn't fishing for you to do that." She met his gaze squarely.

He gave her a rueful smile. "I know. You probably would be the least likely person I know to, um, fish."

"Thank you," she murmured, but then went on determinedly. "But you don't really know anything about me. I could be a—a liar or a gossip or involved in bank robberies."

She frowned when he laughed softly. "Bank embezzlement? Ella, *sei se gut*—we all have our secrets, but I trust that you are not out to commit federal crimes."

She smiled, but felt sad inside when she remembered how much her uncle had taken from her father . . . indeed, from her.

"What is it?"

She almost jumped in her chair as she sought something to say. "Nothing. I—I was wondering what dark secrets you might have . . ." Her words were teasing but she was surprised by the sudden somber expression on his handsome face.

She heard him draw a deep breath, and then his gaze locked with her own. "Maybe I'm not what you think, Ella . . ."

* * *

He watched her brown eyes widen a bit, but she sat still, listening.

Well, he thought. *Here we geh. If I tell her about my past, then she'll run from me, but what woman wouldn't?* He snapped back to the moment and struggled to find the words to begin. "Ella—I—in the past, when I was living with my Amish community—I was accused of a crime and shunned because of it."

He watched a pulse beat in her white throat and felt shaken, but then she spoke.

"So maybe you're a murderer?"

Chapter Seven

She walked alone with him in the dark back to Millie's, and the cadence of his words seemed to match the sound of their steps on the brick pathway.

A murderer . . . a murderer . . . maybe he's a . . .

"Are you?" she asked him finally, trying to see his face in the dim beam of the flashlight he'd turned on.

He seemed to know exactly what she was asking and answered after what seemed like an eternity to Ella. "*Nee* . . . but I was made to feel like one, and when I was shunned, I thought as though I understood what a man who kills another must feel—the guilt, the uncertainty of whether his own life is worth living . . . Of course, I sound like an idiot, but it was so strange and isolating . . . I don't know."

"May I ask what happened?" she asked softly.

"I think you can ask me anything, Ella, and I'll try to answer. In the case of the murder—one of my very best friends was killed as he slept. Dan . . . that was his name . . . The local bishop was coming through the woods and saw me covered in blood. He named me the murderer without any true proof, and I was shunned."

She thought for a moment and then the words tumbled out of her mouth. "I'd still be your friend, Stephen. Shunned or not."

He laughed softly. "*Danki*, Ella. I think that admission deserves a kiss."

She was unprepared for the sudden swooping of his mouth and turned her head slightly. It was both awkward and wonderful; his kiss landed on her cheek, and she had the sudden burning desire for it to be more—much more. She felt her heart pound fast in her chest and was glad that it was dark so that he couldn't see the secret smile she knew was on her lips. It was strange—his kiss stirred something in her that was both fast and wondrous and also something she didn't recognize from her limited experience with Jeremy. She wished he'd stop and talk in the dark, but he'd pulled away and resumed walking.

She fell back into step with him, then thought of something else. "You've never asked me—about my darkest secret—this baby and how it came to be."

"I told you that it doesn't matter to me."

"But maybe it should. I mean, I work at Millie's; I could be a prosti—"

He stopped still and she nearly ran into him. "Don't finish that word. However you got pregnant, I don't believe that it was because you were . . . that."

"So you judge the girls at Millie's?"

"*Nee*, but I know you're different somehow. I don't think you'd . . . give yourself . . . unless you were truly in love."

"Well," she whispered. "I thought I was, but his love turned out to be a sham, an illusion, and I bought it because—because I suppose I simply wanted to be loved."

She felt him run his fingers gently up and down her

right arm. "And you deserve to be loved; to be honored and cherished . . . maybe we all do."

"Oh, I don't know," she whispered. "Sometimes I wonder if God really cares if we are loved."

"I understand how you can feel that way, but I believe He does care—it's just the world that's screwed up."

She half laughed, then sobered as she said what she'd never had the chance to say to anyone. "Well, I miss my father so badly—he was kind and loving, but my mother died when I was born, and I suppose I've always felt like I needed more love to fill up the space left by her loss— or simply a mother's loss. Is your mother still with you?"

She wondered at the strange quiet that followed her words but then she heard him sigh. "*Jah*, you could say that."

She was about to ask him to explain further when he caught her fingers in his own. "You will be a *gut* mother, Ella. I know it—I sense it. And that matters a lot."

She hoped he'd accompany his kind words with another kiss, but instead he caught her hand in his and started to walk again, leaving her hungry for more of his words and the touch of his lips . . .

"So, our dear Mrs. Broom informs me that you entertained a girl from Millie's up here in my unfortunate absence?"

Nick smiled at him, but Stephen wasn't in the mood to play games. "So I did. What about it?"

Nick poured himself two fingers of whiskey and sat down by the embers of the fire. "You need to talk, my friend."

"I need to go to bed."

"But isn't that where you've already been tonight? Bed or bedding or whatever you Amish call it . . ."

"I didn't have her, all right? It's not like that." Against his better judgment, Stephen flung himself into a chair and stared broodingly at the half-empty hot toddy glass that Ella had left behind. He reached out and thumbed the rim of the glass, thinking of her lips and—

"So, what is it?" Nick asked, breaking into his pleasant thoughts. "I've never seen you interested in a girl beyond a passing fancy. What is it about Ella—um—Nichols—pregnant Ella Nichols—that holds such allure for you?"

Stephen resisted the healthy urge to punch his friend and shook his head instead. "I don't know. She's—she's in my blood somehow. Her and the babe. I told her that I don't care who was before, what was before . . . I just . . . I don't know . . . I want to take care of her."

"What if she can take care of herself? Which, I might add, she has done for at least five months of the pregnancy. And she could probably go on with whatever comes her way . . . Look, Steve, I don't want to see you get hurt, that's all."

"Why would I get hurt?"

"Because as far as I know, you've only been with that sweet young widow who used to live around here. I remember that you were quite shaken when she left to go back to her folks. You wanted to take care of her, too, didn't you?"

"Not like this—Laura knew how to stand on her own, with or without me."

"And Ella doesn't? It seems to me that any pregnant woman who'd jump out of a burning building into a stranger's arms can pretty much take care of herself."

Stephen was beginning to feel frustrated, but he kept a tight rein on his temper as he considered Nick's words.

"Look, Steve—I'm no Freudian doctor, but I'd like to suggest that assuming the ready-made care of a woman with baby on board saves you a lot of trouble in the relationship department."

"How so?"

"Because you don't have to think or concentrate or—do whatever courtship rituals you Amish have to do . . . Ella literally jumped into your arms, and again, I think you could get hurt without really taking time to get to know her and allowing her to know you."

Stephen gave him a sour smile and hauled himself out of the chair. "Too late, Nick. I'm already hurt—I'd never be the same if something happened to her . . ."

Nick shook his head. "You've got a bad case, my friend. What happens when she finds out about your past?"

Stephen smiled and gave a slight bow before he sauntered across the floor. "No worries, Nick, she accepts me—murderer or not."

Stephen had the satisfaction of seeing shock and disbelief on his friend's face before he went to bed.

"And where have you been?" Sasha inquired coyly as she opened the door to Ella's knock.

"A boy fell in the pond in town and I needed to help with his rescue."

"Well—" Sasha grinned. "I've heard it called many things, but never a pond rescue."

Ella blinked, then decided to ignore the other girl's insinuations. "I'll go to bed now."

Sasha caught her arm. "Not so fast, pretty pregnant housekeeper—Miss Millie wants to see you in the library."

"Thank you, Sasha." Ella pointedly removed the other girl's hand from her arm and wearily headed for the library—a room filled with well-read books, some leather bound and others simply paperback. Miss Millie did her accounts and reading in the carefully dusted room. She sat behind a huge mahogany desk that had carved lion's paws at its base—it really was a man's desk, but it suited Miss Millie's dominating nature perfectly.

Ella opened the large white door with its brass handle and peeked inside.

"Come in, Ella. There are some things I need to go over with you for next week."

Ella thought of her comfortable bed and longed to put her feet up, but she knew Miss Millie's "going over" of things usually meant a good hour of instructions or additional housekeeping duties. As it was, the basic cleaning and changing of bed linens was exhausting in itself, but she needed the job and now forced herself to listen attentively to the older woman.

"The gentlemen from the fire company will be here at the weekend. A bachelor party for the chief . . . I want to go over the menus and your serving attire. And speaking of what you're wearing, you look rather damp. I don't buy those gray uniform dresses for you to go traipsing about the countryside in them."

"I helped rescue a little boy who fell in a pond." Ella was too tired to go on with any details, and Miss Millie must have sensed that she was working with a waning attention span, so she produced several notepads and pushed them across the desk.

"You'll see that it's a buffet—quite elaborate, I think.

I'll have Mrs. Rob in to cook as usual, but I expect you to oversee things. And I'd like you to wear a nicer dress rather than your regular uniform."

"Why do I need to dress up?" Ella asked blankly, thinking of all the preparatory housekeeping she'd have to do for the event.

Miss Millie smiled faintly. "To tell you the truth, Ella, it's because you seem to have caught the fancy of one of the firefighters, and I think he'd pay just to look at you in a pretty gown."

Ella felt herself flush. "He's my friend, that's all."

"Don't be silly. What better basis to build upon than friendship? I've slept with more friends over the years than I can count—it rather solidifies things, if you take my meaning." For a brief moment, Ella thought she detected a note of regret in Miss Millie's voice, but then decided that she'd been mistaken as the older woman continued.

"I've hired Mrs. Rob's two daughters from town to help as well with preparations and serving . . . Now go to bed before you fall asleep in that chair."

Ella nodded, took the notepads, and went to her comfortable bedroom. She undressed slowly, thinking back over the night's amazing happenings and seeing in her mind's eye the many facets of Stephen. Stephen, fireman protector trying to outswim her to save a boy's life; Stephen, admitting he knew about the pregnancy and still accepting her anyway as a friend; and then the way he'd talked about love and his startling kiss on the road home. She hugged these images of him to her as she nestled into bed. In a way, for the first time since she'd known about her pregnancy, she didn't feel alone that night. *Somehow, Stephen and I have a connection, one that feels like the*

sun and stars . . . She smiled at the fanciful notion but
knew also that there was truth in the analogy, because when
she was with Stephen, things felt balanced somehow—
even down to his darkest secret and the idea of his being
an innocent man accused of murder while her secret pulsed
with new life . . . She closed her eyes and slipped into the
most untroubled sleep she'd had in a long while . . .

Chapter Eight

Stephen returned to the firehouse the next day and unpacked his knapsack with pleasure, glad for the moment to be out of Nick's teasing company. The firehouse had been built in 1922, when the only equipment had been a horse-drawn water tank with a true dalmatian that raced to rescue the townsfolk from fires. Now the Coudersport Firehouse stood strong after a 1957 renovation and the acquisition of an engine and ladders that were the modern face of firefighting.

"Hey, Steve?" Joe called from the camp-like kitchen. Big Joe was a good-hearted giant of a man who never turned away from danger.

"Yeah." Stephen walked into the room and breathed in the good scent of bacon frying.

"There's some kid out front who wants to see you—he's out there petting Midnight."

"All right."

Stephen walked past the fire engine to where a few of the men were sitting out in front of the fire station, enjoying the relaxed moment and the fine morning air. At least ten men were on active duty at the firehouse at any one time and they all got along well together.

Stephen recognized the boy from the pond, amazed at the child's resiliency and further that the huge black dog was allowing the child close enough to pet him. "Jackie Toole?" Stephen smiled and bent down to shake the small hand extended to him. "Shouldn't you still be in bed?"

"Nope. Ma said to run over here and give you this— it's for you and the lady who pulled me out of the pond." The boy fished in his pants pocket and brought out a crumpled letter that had obviously been white earlier but was now stained with childish fingerprints.

Stephen opened the note and read carefully between the sticky traces of bubblegum. "Why, it's a dinner invitation for Miss Nichols and me . . . That's great!" He ruffled Jackie's hair. "You tell your mother that I'm on call, but I'll let Miss Nichols know and we'll be there come Wednesday night as long as we're able."

"Thank you." The boy nodded, stroked Midnight's ear, and then was off like a shot across the road toward town.

That kid'll probably need to be rescued more times than not before he grows up . . . Stephen smiled to himself, glad that he had an excuse to see Ella again. He needed to invite her to the Tooles' dinner and hopefully could escort her there himself. He started to whistle and walked back into the station, passing Big Joe as he turned the bacon in a huge frying pan.

"Smells good, Joe."

"Thanks. I'm aiming for some pancakes here too."

Stephen smiled at his friend's deft turning of the food. It was Big Joe who'd first introduced him to the firehouse and who'd secured him a job with the crew.

"Hey, where you going, Steve? Breakfast's almost ready!"

"Keep something warm for me, will you, Joe? I've got to run a quick errand out to Miss Millie's."

"Miss Millie's?" Joe hollered after him. "At this time of day?"

"Yep!" Stephen smiled and hurried out the back door of the station.

Ella pulled the white sheet through the wringer washer and sighed to herself. It was wash day—which meant nearly a whole morning doing sheets and bedding, as well as delicates for the girls. Still, the back garden of Millie's was a secret delight to the senses in the bright morning sunshine. The smell of lilacs and budding roses welcomed the bumblebees that had ventured out to work, and Ella felt a companionship with the little creatures which kept her spirits up as she washed.

She was so absorbed in cranking the wringer that she nearly jumped in surprise when Stephen spoke to her. "Why are you doing this?"

"Aren't you going to say good morning?" she asked sweetly as she continued to work. She glanced at him briefly, long enough to take in his ruffled dark hair and eyes that appeared more blue today than green . . . *Probably because he's wearing a blue shirt . . .*

"Ella?"

"Hmmm?"

"This is too hard a job for you to be doing in your condition."

She shushed him quickly. "Don't say that too loud—there are windows open in the house, and I need this job. I'm managing just fine."

She heard him make an exasperated sound, and then he took the end of the wet sheet from her. "All right . . . well, I'm going to help you."

"You can't . . . Someone might see you and tell Millie I'm not up to the work."

He grabbed the crank handle, and she grabbed his arm, but it didn't do any good. It was like trying to move a tree trunk. "Stephen!" she hissed in frustration and opened her mouth to further protest. His kiss caught her unawares once more, but soon melted all resistance from her. *He smells so good . . . so right for me . . . like sunshine and heat and the mountains . . .* She shivered with pleasure when he let the wet sheet drop between them. It clung to her tingling breasts and dampened the blue of his shirt. She made a small sound from the back of her throat and she sensed that it pushed him beyond some veiled restraint . . .

She pulsed with life . . . He felt her on so many levels—body, soul, spirit . . . And he wanted to get closer, like a thirsting man to a fountainhead. He let his tongue trace the contours of her mouth, then slowly began to kiss down her neck and into the heady warmth of her shoulder. His hands ached to find the tight fullness of her breasts, but he rocked hard against her instead, holding her to him until he was sure she could feel his body through the press of skirt, sheet, and pants.

"Oh, Stephen . . ." she whispered, and he wanted to swing her up into his arms and carry her into the grove of lilacs and make love to her right there. But he vaguely registered that the house behind them had eyes and that Ella was no strumpet to be used and tossed aside . . . *Yet she had been—by the father of her babe . . .* The chilling thought cooled his ardor a bit, and he pulled away from her long enough to stare down into her flushed face. Her lips looked red and slightly swollen and he realized that she shared the same tumultuous passion that he did, especially when she reached for him and breathed his name once more.

"Oh, Stephen, indeed." Sasha's voice was saccharine sweet and had the effect of someone dumping ice water down his back. He pressed close to Ella, unwilling to reveal his arousal to the other girl's bold gaze, but Sasha ran a fingernail down his sweat-soaked shirt, and he grimaced at the touch.

"Sasha, let us be." Ella's voice had a tired edge to it, which made Stephen all the more frustrated. He straightened finally and turned to look down at Sasha.

"What is it that you want?" he growled.

"No, pretty man, what is it that *you* want? Because if it's what you've been doing with our housekeeper, I'll have to get Millie to set you up a tab." The girl smirked, and Stephen set his jaw. He resented what the girl was implying, even though it lined up with his own thinking of only a few minutes before. He didn't let the incongruity bother him though as he spoke in clear tones to Ella.

"The Tooles have invited us to dinner on Wednesday evening to thank us for saving Jackie. I'll see you about five p.m. unless something interferes . . ." He let his gaze brush coldly over Sasha, then took his leave from the garden.

He hated to think of Ella finishing the mountain of laundry by herself but realized that he'd probably only cause her more trouble if he went back. He walked to the station in a subdued frame of mind, trying to understand how quickly he lost control with Ella Nichols . . .

Ella entered the kitchen later that morning to find Mrs. Rob, a comfortable-looking woman from town, already hard at work baking ham and making piecrusts for the coming party. "Now," the older woman chirped cheerfully, "you sit right down and have some tea before you do anything else, Miss Ella. Tea is good for a mother's constitution."

"You know about the baby?" Ella asked, accepting the tall, cool glass of tea with gratitude. "And you don't have to call me 'miss'—I fear it would only upset Miss Millie and some of the other girls."

"Well, it'll just be between us, then, because I know a lady when I see one—though how ya came to be here, I'll never understand, and I won't pry none neither about the babe."

"Thank you," Ella murmured.

"Oh and my two eldest girls will be around later as well, though I wouldn't want them to get any ideas once they've seen the inside of this place—Miss Millie sure turns a good hand at business—beggin' yer pardon, Miss Ella."

"No." Ella smiled faintly. "She does run the club well."

Ella watched the older woman's hands move with wonderful dexterity as she crimped a piecrust, then quickly moved on to another. "I'll freeze these crusts once they've baked and cooled and then all we'll have to do is fill them the day of . . ."

Ella put down her tea glass and reached for a bowl of bright green peas that needed shelling. She still had to clean the two front bedrooms as well as the water closet near the second-floor landing. *And then I'll have to talk to Miss Millie about getting off work at five p.m. on Wednesday* . . . She was filled with secret delight at the chance to see Stephen again and snapped the peas through her fingers without truly seeing them as she recalled his early-morning kisses . . .

"Ella?"

She realized that Mrs. Rob must have repeated her name several times, and she looked up, feeling herself flush. "Yes—I'm sorry."

"No need to be sorry, child. Not when you're lovestruck. I wanted to know if you needed help finishing those peas."

"Lovestruck?" Ella queried. *Is that what I am about Stephen? Lovestruck and moony-eyed?*

"See what I mean?" Mrs. Rob asked with a dimpled smile.

Ella nodded, but couldn't bring herself to answer. *Am I falling in love again when only five months ago I thought I loved Jeremy? I've got to get a rein on my emotions . . .* Against her will, she recalled meeting Jeremy for the first time. She'd been strolling along the promenade of small shops in Cape May, looking for a birthday gift for her father, and her handbag had caught on the arm of a male passerby. It was then that she'd looked into Jeremy's eyes and felt her world go off-kilter. He seemed to devour her with his gaze, and she'd felt both fear and excitement, though she'd thought that the initial fear was merely the thrill of falling in love at first sight. *But now I know better . . . as I should have known then. And maybe I should be more careful with Stephen now . . .*

She returned to shelling peas with sober vigor.

Chapter Nine

The Toole family home was bursting at the seams with boisterous children—Jackie being the youngest of ten sons. Stephen found the plethora of boyish clutter to be cheerful—baseball gloves, pet frogs, gumdrops, and cap guns—all seemed to litter every possible flat surface except the long wooden slab of a dining table, carefully set with tin plates and cups. It was by no means a grand home, but it exuded happiness, and Stephen felt a pull in his heart's memory when he compared his own cold upbringing to the lively bustle of the Tooles' house. In his Amish home, he could remember no laughter, few toys, and the meagerness of meals . . . It had been a place that had brought ingrained desolation to his soul . . .

He pushed his dark thoughts away as he glanced across the madcap kitchen to see Ella watching the antics of the children with a soft smile on her mouth. He let his gaze drop to her belly and knew instinctively that she would be a good mother—especially if she enjoyed the ordered chaos of the Toole family as much as she seemed to be doing.

He was about to cross the room to her when Mrs. Toole let out an effective bellow. "Supper's on!"

Stephen was almost run over by the herd of boys, but finally managed to secure seats for Ella and himself at the end of one long bench, to the right of Mr. Toole.

The family bowed their heads with one accord while Mr. Toole thanked God for the food, his wife, his children, and their guests. Stephen wondered when it was that he'd last heard someone pray for him out loud, then pushed the thought aside as a bowl of mountainous mashed potatoes was passed his way. Roast chicken, stuffing, and green beans soon followed in quick succession, as well as whole-berry cranberry sauce, a broccoli cheese casserole, and warm angel biscuits.

One of the older scamps peered down the table and was studying Ella with something akin to awe, and Stephen remarked on it with a smile. "What are you thinking, son?"

The boy withstood a general outburst of teasing laughter from his siblings, then spoke up boldly. "Jest thinkin' that Jackie wouldna be here if it weren't fer her, and I don't care if she does work down at the Social Club neither."

Stephen knew Ella's discomfiture even without looking at her. He reached beneath the table and gave her knee a reassuring squeeze. He was about to speak when Mrs. Toole banged her spoon upon the table. "Jimmy, watch yer mouth! Pa! Don't you have somethin' to say to the boy?"

Mr. Toole, a genial, quiet fellow, opened his eyes wide and peered down the table. "Why yes, Ma. I'm askin' these fine folks here to come to Bible study tonight with us at the church."

"Pa! You ain't thinkin' straight, but you are thinkin'

right. I should have said so myself! Would you like ta come? Mr. Stephen? Miss Ella?"

Stephen was about to decline, thinking that Ella would probably prefer her privacy, but to his surprise, she looked at him with a smile on her lips. "Do you mind if we go, Stephen?"

"Uh . . . sure! Thank you, Mrs. Toole. We'd love to . . ."

"Aw, jest call me Ma! Everyone else round here does."

"All right—Ma—thank you."

Stephen continued with his meal thoughtfully. He hadn't had much to do with the Bible since he'd left the mountain, and he had no idea what Ella believed. *I wish she was Amish . . .* He stared down at his potatoes, startled by the quiet whisper of a thought. *Why care if she's Amish or not . . . ? I haven't had much to do with my faith or living by the Ordnung lately, so why should it matter . . . ?* And then, like a groundswell, it hit him hard between a mouthful of cranberries and one of broccoli—*I really care for her and the baby . . .* He dropped his fork and glanced at Ella, half afraid that she might read his thoughts. *Friends . . . We are just friends . . . And I am losing my mind to this girl . . .* He came back to the moment abruptly, realizing that Ma was insisting he try her peach cobbler. He let Ella serve him, and he was warmly fascinated as he watched her slender hands move. Then he shook his head and let the smooth richness of the cobbler ease down his throat while his heart still beat out E-L-L-A like the tattoo of Ma Toole's spoon.

Ella hadn't been to a church since her father's funeral. In truth, she'd been angry with God then, and the remnants of that anger still tore at her. But her father had taught her, from a young age, that running from God in anger or sorrow would do no good; God would pursue you because of His great love. She recalled now that these were the words that had been spoken over her father's coffin, which had been set up in the front room of the Glass Castle. He had died so suddenly of pneumonia that Ella had had little to no time to grieve . . . It was little wonder that she had sought Jeremy and the baby as a refuge of sorts . . .

All of these words of her father now came rushing back into her mind as she sat beside Stephen in the small church pew. The Tooles and other townsfolk were gathered, and the place was lit cozily by lantern light—the better to save on the electric bill, the young pastor had joked upon meeting her. The small, wood-floored church was the only place of worship in the poorer part of town, and Ella realized it might not be well supported, at that. The young pastor looked nervous to her, and she wondered if he was new at the job, but then Lester Pike came in slowly, and the man at the pulpit seemed to take on fresh courage as he began the study.

"We want to welcome our guests this evening—I'm Pastor Rook, and I'm glad to see you all here. Tonight, we're taking a look at a few verses about faith . . ."

Ella watched Stephen take a Bible from the pew back, and his tanned slender fingers found the passage with the ease of familiarity. She was grateful when he moved closer that they might share and she breathed in his scent—something like the mountains and wilderness. It made her feel comforted, almost the way she'd felt when he'd caught her from the flames; but there was also something primal about him that caused her belly to tighten and her mouth to sting.

I must be crazy, and we're in a church too . . . Ella

dragged her attention back to the pastor and began to truly listen.

"You might vacation somewhere—say somewhere near the sea. And every morning you get up and find yourself studying the beautiful waves as they pound against the shore." Pastor Rook's voice was pleasant, but he captured the image of the roaring waves in Ella's mind. "And then one morning you get up to find that a vast fog has rolled in and the sea is no longer visible. Now, you don't say to yourself, 'The sea is gone.' You know it's there with only a temporal blocking of its view . . . Well, so it is with faith in God. Sometimes when the fogs of life, of disappointment, of regret or fear cloud our vision, we might think that God—Who commands the sea—is no longer there. That He has left us. But God wants us to trust Him, even if we cannot see His power working in our lives. He longs for us to call out 'I know you're there, God—even though things seem dark right now and I cannot see you.'" Pastor Rook cleared his throat. "Please bow your heads with me for a few moments of silent reflection."

Ella closed her eyes, and for the first time in a very long time, she felt enveloped by God's love and she knew a great thankfulness in her heart. She realized that she had lost faith in God for much too long—first with her father's sudden death, then the cruelty of her uncle, and then Jeremy's merciless attitude toward the baby she carried. Yet here, in this little church, she found that perhaps God had never left her after all. She felt Stephen slide his hand over hers, and she understood instinctively that he, too, was not unaffected by the pastor's simple but profound story.

The pastor then gave a final blessing, and Ella rose to make her way across and down the aisle, only to find

Lester Pike at her elbow in the crowd. "Good evening, Mr. Pike," she said gaily. "Did you enjoy the service?"

"Aw, now, I imagine I did—I could understand about the fog with my blindness and all."

Ella was about to murmur something polite when Stephen caught the old man's hand. "You see beyond physical sight, my friend. And I've only known one other in my life who could do such a thing. Thank you, Lester—for being you."

Ella wondered whom Stephen spoke of but then she was swept up in a throng of Toole boys and she forgot about her questioning thought, simply pleased to feel Stephen at her back and her heart lighter than it had been in weeks . . .

Mitch eased out of the shadows of the church, waiting until everyone was gone. He didn't know what had brought him to the service—something about the lantern light and a long-forgotten memory of sitting on his mother's lap—being held, being loved. Then the pastor's carrying words about God . . . *What has God ever done for me? He left me alone with my father. He saw how I was beaten and He didn't care. He saw that I was naked and afraid and hungry and broken and He didn't care* . . . Mitch nearly jumped out of his skin when a voice behind him spoke softly.

"That was quite a nice service tonight. I liked the lantern light."

Mitch turned and faced Lester Pike. "You're blind. How could you see the light?" Mitch demanded, preparing to walk off.

"I can," Lester assured him. "But I know it's hard when

other things cloud my mind—bad memories, things that seem unfair, my mother dying in a car accident . . ."

Mitch kicked hard at the ground. "So what? You had some trouble . . . you seem fine now. I bet nobody ever beat you when you was little."

"No," Lester agreed sadly. "But God still loves you, and He—"

"That don't explain nuthin'," Mitch choked. "Why would a good God let a little fella be treated so bad? Huh? Tell me!"

Mitch watched the old man shake his head. "Man sins. But God is still good. He is love that is real to help us through the tough times and—"

"Shut up! Jest shut up! All you're saying is that you don't really know, and that makes you a liar! Do you hear me? A liar, and your God is nuthin' but a cheat . . ." Mitch backed away from Lester and started to move down the street. He told himself that the stupid old man could find his way home easy enough, but that he had a job to finish . . .

Stephen held her hand as he walked her back to Millie's; it seemed easy, natural, and he was feeling relaxed after this night's time in church.

"I had fun at the Tooles'," he confided as a silent symphony of lightning bugs cascaded around them.

"Yes, it would be wonderful to have so many chil—" She broke off, as if she were embarrassed.

And he finished gently. "Children?"

"Yes."

"I can only agree." He resisted the urge to pull her closer, because he wanted those children, wanted to be their father and Ella their mother . . . *I'm* narrish . . . *but*

I want it with her so badly I can taste it . . . Sei se gut, Gott, *make it real and bless Ella and the* boppli *she carries . . .*

He did hug her closer to his side then and felt, for once, that he might be happy . . .

Mitch was dreaming. *His father was screaming and chasing him with a wooden baseball bat. Mitch knew his child's legs could not outrun his father, and his own screams soon echoed through the woods. Mitch felt the harsh grasp at his neck and kicked his legs, trying to break free when he looked down and saw a small baby in his arms. The baby cried out too, and Mitch longed to comfort it, but then he realized that his father had let him go. He cradled the baby in his chubby arms and turned to look behind him. His father was gone, and all that remained was a warm light—warm to help the baby . . . He walked toward the warmth and watched the baby stop crying. He heard his own breathing, still fast and hard, but he was free . . . the baby had saved him . . .*

Mitch woke and heard the cries coming from the back of his throat. He sat up fast and realized he was drenched with sweat. He put his head in his hands, and his dream replayed itself again behind his eyes. He started to cry and brushed angrily at the tears, but then he let them go and sobbed into the tangled sheet. *The baby . . . The baby had saved him . . .*

Chapter Ten

Ella adjusted the simple white collar on the pretty blue dress that Miss Millie had given her. She studied herself in the mirror and decided to pile her red hair into a neat chignon. Her new dress fitted tightly in the bodice, then flared outward with a flounce of petticoats. Silk stockings and uncomfortable high heels completed the look, and she felt a slight thrill of excitement as she considered what Stephen's reaction might be when he saw her. She'd never dressed so provocatively before in her life, and she was glad that her stomach was feeling nicely settled after a quick meal of toast and applesauce. The petticoats hid her pregnancy, and she reminded herself that she was too quickly becoming involved with another good-looking man . . . *And where did it get me the last time? But something seems different about Stephen . . .*

A quick knock on her door brought her musings to an end, and she left the room to help Mrs. Rob arrange the trays of canapés that were to be circulated among the guests before the buffet was revealed.

* * *

Stephen smiled faintly when the chief gave him a hearty slap on the back. The men were walking together with a dozen or so others and had left behind a disappointed skeleton crew at the station. The men had good-naturedly drawn straws to see who had to stay behind at the station while the rest laughed and talked as they made their way down the streets to Miss Millie's. Stephen didn't try to suppress the excitement he felt knowing that he might see Ella. He had every intention of seeking her out, no matter her duties of housekeeping. He gave half his attention to the talk surrounding him while reflecting on the kiss in the garden with the wet sheets. The linen had clung to her gray dress like a second skin, lying sleekly across the rapid rise and fall of her high breasts. He half shook his head, realizing that he was becoming obsessed with the girl, but it felt so good and . . .

"Hey, Steve!" Joe's booming voice penetrated his reverie, and he gave his big friend a surprised look. "Where's your head, Steve? We're here already."

Stephen smiled and drew a deep breath as he mounted the outside stairs to the gracious porch. The big door was opened by a tall redhead who drew low whistles of appreciation from the men—all but Stephen himself. *Where did she get that fancy dress . . . ?* His adrenaline was running fast and he could feel the throb of his pulse as he shouldered past Mike and Joe to slide his arms around Ella.

"What are you doing?" he whispered hoarsely in her shell-like ear, ignoring the catcalls at his back.

"Opening the door to greet our guests." She spoke through gritted teeth, though she smiled widely as he backed away a bit but still kept one arm proprietarily around her blue sateen waist.

"Gentlemen," he said with a laugh in his throat as he

turned to face his friends. "Forgive me, but I think I've found my—uh—entertainment for the evening."

"Then let us pass," Joe called good-naturedly. "So we can do the same."

Stephen pulled Ella gently out of the way, only to have her slip from his arms and whisper irritably up at him, "If anyone sees what you're doing, I will lose my job. I'm the house—"

He interrupted her torrent of words by swooping down and kissing her hard, using his tongue, then his teeth against her lips. Then he broke away and spun her around to face a well-dressed Miss Millie.

"Well, my dear—I told you that a pretty dress would pay off, didn't I? And you, sir—I'm afraid Ella needs to help attend to serving our guests tonight."

Stephen smiled at the older woman. "How much to have her—serve me for the evening?" He felt Ella stiffen beneath his arm but didn't care.

"You'd be making me scramble to get help, young man," Miss Millie pointed out in a teasing tone.

Stephen saw Mike approaching with a girl on each arm and spoke quickly. "Name your price. I know she'll be well worth it . . ."

Ella longed to box his ears, though her lips still stung with the hard caress of his mouth. It was positively degrading and oddly exciting at the same time to listen to his deep voice purchase her time like he was bidding on cattle. But she was oddly sure that his offer of money was based on some plan to keep her out of hand's reach of the other men.

Finally, Miss Millie was satisfied, and Stephen bent

down to nuzzle Ella's neck and then whisper against her throat, "Where's your room?"

"On the third floor—it's hot," she murmured back, wondering how far he planned to take this game.

"*Kumme*," he said simply, pulling her to the ornate staircase. He kept his arm around her waist as they mounted the steps, much to the cheering delight of his fellow firemen.

When they'd gained the second landing, the noise from below had faded and Stephen stepped away from her. She saw, much to her surprise, that his handsome cheeks were flushed with color.

"Look, I apologize for my behavior down there. I have no right to try and control what you do."

"No, you don't," she muttered, then rubbed absently at her rib cage, encased in the blue dress.

"That dress is too tight—among other things."

She found herself smiling up at him. "Would you promise to turn your back while I change it?"

"*Jah*," he said simply.

"Then let's go to my room."

He nodded and she let him follow her up the claret-colored carpeted stairs.

She was a bit breathless by the time they'd reached her door. It was hot on the third floor, but she liked the privacy she had there, and the larger room, since nearly all the girls were on the second floor.

She pulled a key on a red ribbon from her bodice and undid the old-fashioned lock. She held the door wide for him to pass and was unprepared for the slight brush of his tanned forearm against her and the sudden onslaught of feeling his light touch produced. But she straightened her spine and closed the door behind her, pausing to press her back against the solid wood. She watched him prowl the confines of the simply wallpapered room like some restless big cat.

"Sit down," she finally said, indicating the bed. She was frustrated that her voice sounded high and breathy, but she'd never been so intimate with a man, even Jeremy, as to have him sit on her bed. With Jeremy, it had been a deserted boathouse, where the roar of the sea was the only sound. She somehow knew that making love might be drastically different with this Amish man . . .

Stephen sat down carefully on the soft pile of linens and springy mattress beneath. He let his gaze drift over the gentle female intimacies displayed in the room— Ella's stockings and garter belt, casually slung over a button back chair, frothy lace peeking from drawers and crocheted doilies on the dresser tops—the trappings of a woman.

"It must seem strange to you," she said with a note of shyness in her voice.

"What?" he asked.

"All of this." She gestured with a small hand. "Frivolity. I mean—don't Amish women live and dress much more simply?"

"They do," he said slowly. "But every woman has her—secrets." He savored the word, then stretched out his hands and caught her around the waist, drawing her in to the sprawl of his legs.

He expected some protest, but she moved willingly, and he felt his throat tighten with excitement. He slid his hands tenderly over her belly, then raised them to the first blue button of her dress.

"I thought you'd turn your back," she whispered.

"You're not out of the dress yet, *siessherz*—sweetheart."

He let his fingers ease the second button open, and the high curves of her breasts were revealed. He knew by the throb of a pulse at her throat and the rapid rise and fall of her chest that she was excited. *But I've got to be a gentleman here . . . She's pregnant . . .* He swallowed hard and dropped his hands to her waist once more as the thought beat around his brain . . . *She can't get any more pregnant . . . It would be so easy . . .*

He stood up abruptly, then bent to quickly kiss her mouth, seeking to leave the torture of the soft bed and her soft body, but she teetered on her high heels, then fell fully against him. He found himself on his back in the embracing mattress with Ella sprawled atop him. He couldn't suppress the groan that came from the back of his throat as she scrambled to get off, but she only made the tight situation worse by sending a shocking knee into his groin.

He literally saw stars, but they soon faded in the lamplight as she hovered close, asking if he was all right, her dark eyes twin secrets of delight. She bent nearer and he arched his neck, unable to do anything else with her mouth in such proximity. The kiss was long and intoxicating. He forgot reserve, restraint, as his fingers cupped her face to position in for his kiss. He was intent on running his tongue across her lips when she suddenly grew pale. He moved fast, sitting up with her and snatching a lined wicker waste bin from the floor just in time.

He rubbed her back and held the escaped loose tendrils of red hair from the mass on her head. When the storm had passed, he handed her his handkerchief, and she wiped her mouth slowly before lifting her head to stare into his eyes.

"I'm sorry," she whispered miserably.

"For being pregnant?" He leaned forward and pressed his lips against the freckles on her pale cheek. "Don't be."

After a minute, he eased her down into the bed, carefully arranging the pillows behind her back. "You change that dress and I'll go get you a drink, all right?"

He watched her nod, then he turned from the bed and headed to the door. It surprised him, how much she shook him. Feelings at core level, primal and deep, always seemed to surface when he was near her. *I suppose that's what love feels like* . . . He stopped still on the thick carpet at the striking thought, then pushed it aside, not sure he even knew what love was. He went down the hall to fetch her some fresh water.

Ella changed into one of her plain gray uniform dresses and, feeling rather tired, lay back on the pillows Stephen had arranged. She became drowsily aware that her door was being eased open and was surprised that Stephen had found her a drink so quickly. She sat up straighter in expectation and nearly screamed aloud when a strange man with slicked-back hair and dark clothes entered the room instead.

Mitch had found his way through the maze of the big house and tracked down Ella and the fireman. He'd listened at the door to their talk, then ducked into an alcove when the fireman left the room. Then Mitch had moved to open her door—his head pounding with the adrenaline rushing through him.

She was sitting on the bed, looking tired, but her body tensed up as her eyes met his, and he knew she was about to scream.

"Don't yell—please," he said, his heart pounding in his throat. "I—I just want to talk."

"The party is downstairs," she said coldly, lifting her chin and slowly getting to her feet. "Who are you?"

He admired her tough attitude and again thought about her being pregnant.

"Look, I'll tell you the truth." He held up his hands. "Your uncle and step-aunt sent me."

"Why?" He watched her inch toward the dresser, thinking she probably had some sort of weapon concealed there.

"Don't—don't do anything sudden-like, all right? I didn't know you was pregnant."

She stared at him. "What difference does it make? Who are you?" she demanded again.

"It don't matter who or what I am. But you should know that your uncle and aunt—they're evil and out for ya. And if they knewed ya were pregnant, why, they'd only be out to git ya more."

He watched her put a protective hand against her belly as she straightened her shoulders. "So you're here to take me back to them?"

He wet his lips and said the first truth that came to his mind. "No, but I can't kill no baby."

He had no sooner uttered those words than he felt a tremendous blow to the back of his head. As if in slow motion, he fell to the floor, feeling darkness swallow him.

Chapter Eleven

Stephen felt the blood pound in his temples as he stared down at the man he'd just knocked out with the water pitcher he'd been carrying.

"Are you all right?"

Ella nodded, but he saw her ashen color, and he stepped over the unconscious man to open his arms so she could hurry into his embrace.

"I've never struck another person," he confided on a half laugh. "The Amish are supposed to be a peaceful lot, but when I heard him and what he was saying to you . . . I lost control."

"Should we call the police?" Ella asked him with a shiver as the man started to move.

"Not yet," Stephen said, moving her carefully away from the stranger. "I want him to talk about your *aenti* and *onkel*. He may clam up if we get the police."

Once Ella was safely on the other side of the room, Stephen hauled the damp man into a chair and waited for him to come around.

It didn't take long before the man was groaning and clutching his head. But the words he spoke while his eyes were still closed echoed in the room. "The baby—save the baby."

"You said you came from Ella's uncle and aunt . . . why?" Stephen watched the man's eyes slowly focus.

"They paid me to do a job—to kill the girl."

Stephen struggled to restrain himself as he glanced at Ella, then back to the stranger. Stephen longed to pummel the man again but needed more information.

"I set the fire at the boardinghouse and saw you bring her down the ladder."

"That's arson and attempted murder—federal crimes," Stephen bit out.

"I know . . . but I couldn't kill no baby. I was there that night on the road by the pond . . . that Lester Pike—he told me things about God . . . Anyways, I'm done. Turn me in."

Stephen looked at Ella. "Is there anything else you want to know?"

"Yes . . . My aunt and uncle want me killed . . . Is it— about the letter and the will I took from my uncle's study?"

The man nodded his head. "Yeah . . . I think so . . . And I know they won't stop—even if I go in the slammer. They won't stop, and there's no place you can hide from them."

"I know a place," Stephen said grimly "I know a place where you and the baby will be safe . . ."

PART II

ICE MOUNTAIN, 1958

Chapter Twelve

The filtered sunlight of a summer's afternoon cast both shadow and light on Ella's face as she sat on the wagon seat next to Stephen. They were headed away from Coudersport, high up into the mountains, on a road that had long since ceased to be macadam.

"What will they say? What will they think of me being pregnant?" Ella knew that her questions had increased the closer they got to what Stephen called the Ice Mine, but he merely focused on the reins of the wagon, handling them with easy dexterity, and gave her what she considered to be a forced smile from his beautiful mouth. When he spoke, his words were measured. "You'll be safe, Ella, and Joel Umble—the spiritual leader of the community—is my friend."

"How long has it been since you've seen him?" She was nervous, but her temperament made her curious as well. "Did he stick by you when—when they thought you had killed someone?"

She watched him lower his dark head, then finally lift his chin to stare straight ahead at the road. "*Jah*, Joel did . . . and Martha, his wife. But—my family did not."

"I'm sorry," she said instantly. "I know how that must have felt. My own family, after my father died, turned against me . . . My uncle was . . . cruel, to say the least, but to think he wants to kill me . . . I still don't understand."

She felt Stephen's sharp gaze. "How was he cruel?"

Ella blinked back unexpected tears at the tenderness behind the question and allowed her thoughts to unwind a bit from the tightly held ball she'd kept locked up inside. "I grew up in Cape May, New Jersey—it's a beautiful seaside town full of old Victorian houses . . . I was raised in one called the Sea Glass Castle, or the Glass Castle for short. It was a truly beautiful place with lots of nooks and crannies to hide and read in, and the ocean was only five minutes' walk away . . . My uncle and step-aunt always coveted the place. They tried to buy it from my father many times, but he would never sell—and then my father died when I was seventeen, and they—they managed to take the house and my father's money because I was underage and they were on good terms with a local judge. I lost my home . . . I guess that's how he was cruel."

"I'm sorry, Ella," Stephen said softly. "You do understand what it's like to lose family . . . What about your *mamm*?"

"My mother died when I was born. And—and your dad?"

She heard him sigh briefly; then he shot her a sideways glance. "My *fater* died when I was young—a hunting accident. My mother and her sister raised me, but they were—are—bitter women, and I ran wild in the woods most of the time to avoid their venom. I tried to love them—and maybe I do in some small way. But when I was accused of murder—well, they had more to say about me than other folks who didn't even know me well . . . It was as if suddenly I could see the truth about what they really thought. I couldn't stand it any longer—so I left the mountain."

"And now you're going back to all that—for me?" She reached impulsively to touch his hands on the reins. "Oh, Stephen, turn back around! I'll find another way. I don't want you to be hurt because of me."

He looked square at her then, his now-green eyes intense with something she couldn't fathom. He cleared his throat, then spoke hoarsely. "*Danki*, Ella, for thinking of me . . . but around this bend in the road is the Ice Mine and the little house where they sell tickets to visit the place in the summer . . . And I don't want to turn back— it's a small enough hurt to face to comfort and keep you safe—remember . . . we're friends." His long fingers stroked her own, and then she slid her hand away and nodded.

"All right . . . I remember. Friends."

The scent of the mountain is the first thing that hits you . . . full of richness and mystery and hope . . . Stephen thrust these thoughts away, not wanting to dwell on the beauty of the place where he was raised—it hurt— and he didn't want Ella to see how much returning to Ice Mountain shook him. He turned the horse into the Ellises' stock pen as Mr. Ellis, a jovial *Englischer* who was a great friend to the Amish, came out to assist Ella down, then turned to help Stephen unhitch.

"It's been a while, son. Heard you were working in Coudersport as a firefighter."

Stephen nodded. "Thought I'd take a little break . . ."

Mr. Ellis cast Ella a smiling glance as she stood with her dress blowing and pressed against her in the slight mountain breeze. "You've been busy, Stephen. Do you know when you two are due to deliver?"

Stephen turned and looked at her, and the thought hit him like a lightning bolt. *He thinks Ella's baby is mine . . . Maybe it would be best for everyone on the mountain to think the same . . .* He sought Ella's dark eyes but found no answer there, and he wet his lips before he answered Mr. Ellis. "Busy enough, sir. But I'm not much on dates of delivery—better to just let things happen as they come."

Mr. Ellis clapped him on the shoulder. "Now that's a good answer, son! Do you both have time to see the mine before you head home? The icicles are nearly full grown."

Stephen didn't look at Ella this time but shook his head. "*Nee, danki.* The hike up the mountain will be long for her . . . We'll stop on our way down sometime."

"Good enough." Mr. Ellis briskly started to talk price on putting up the horse and Stephen concentrated on the business and didn't realize when Ella walked away.

Ella was enchanted by the beautiful little white house and attached gift shop. Apparently, many traveled during the summer to see the mine. But an ice mine in late spring or summer? It sounded strange to her, almost miraculous. She took a deep breath of the fragrant air and thought that it seemed like home somehow, then she wandered along the brief path to admire the fern-filled side of the mountain.

"They only grow here, you know."

She whirled to find Stephen close behind her, and she laughed. "Ooh, you scared me. What only grow here, the ferns?"

"Yep. Folks from all over have tried to cultivate them elsewhere, but this variety only thrives on Ice Mountain."

"I can understand why—the air is so full and rich. It reminds me of the sea somehow . . . May we see inside the mine?"

She watched him nod, but sensed that it was something he'd rather not do and quickly changed her mind. "Oh, Stephen, maybe sometime later—I'm sorry. How far is it to your community?"

He smiled then, a flash of white teeth and a stray dimple appearing beside his mouth. She forgot what Jeremy looked like, what any man had ever looked like, as she gazed up into his blue-green eyes, shot through with sunlight. "You want to see the mine—*kumme*. We'll have a quick look."

He took her hand, and she thrilled to his long fingers twining gently through her own and followed him to what seemed to be a thick wooden door, set in the side of the mountain. He lifted the wooden bar across the latch, and a blast of cold air burst forth from within. Ella shivered in delight. He turned up a lantern and held it high as he scooped her close beside him. She wasn't sure if it was the palatial display of ice or his nearness that made her heart thump with delight, but suddenly, most assuredly, she had found a place that rivaled the beauty of the sea.

"Oh," she said on a sigh as she gazed at the magnificent, crystal clear ice. "It's like sea glass."

"Your old home?" he asked softly.

"No—sea glass can be found along the beaches. It's old glass from bottles or dishes that has been polished smooth by the pounding of the water and then washes back ashore."

"As we do in life sometimes," he replied. "*Gott* shapes

something new from the old, broken pieces, and we find ourselves back where we started—washed ashore."

Ella turned beneath his arm, pressing against him instinctively. "But that new shore can be a new beginning." She watched him smile grimly in the light of the lantern and wanted to do something to change his mood. She stretched on tiptoe and gently pressed her lips to his mouth.

Stephen almost dropped the lantern. He was unprepared for the hot rush of feeling that fired through him at the touch of her lips. He caught her close with his free arm and couldn't seem to think rationally, caught between the fused heat of their mouths and the surrounding chill of the ice. The dual sensations were heady fuel for his heart, and he found himself returning her kiss with flagrant delight. He kissed her until he felt her bend over his arm, and then suddenly, it was as if reality crashed into him with one subtle movement . . . He felt the insistent kicking of the babe inside her belly.

"I'm sorry," he muttered roughly as he lowered his arm and set her on her feet.

"Don't be," she said lightly. "I kissed you first."

He noticed she was shivering and took her hand. "*Kumme*, it's too cold in here for you."

"It wasn't a few seconds ago," she mumbled.

"What was that?" He paused as he walked her to the door and decided she'd merely said something about the cold.

Once outside, he blinked in the bright sunlight and looked down at her. "I didn't hurt you or the baby, did I?"

"Not at all. I—liked it."

"*Gut* . . . that's good." He cast about for something more to say, then looked to the mountain and the small path that led upward behind the mine. "I'm afraid there's quite a hike in front of us, but I can carry you, if you'd like."

"Stephen, I'm pregnant, but I can hike. If I get tired, I'll tell you."

He nodded, trying to gauge her response. He wanted no harm to *kumme* to her, and he realized that his heart was starting to follow where his body had begun . . .

Chapter Thirteen

Ella paused to catch her breath beside a blooming mountain laurel, and Stephen shook his dark head.

"That's far enough," he said, and she felt herself being swung easily up into his strong arms.

It was an odd feeling—being carried. It reminded her of the night of the fire and the surety of his arms then . . .

"Relax," he whispered against her hair and she did. She was lulled by the gentle coos of mourning doves and the sound of Stephen's heartbeat as she nestled more cozily against him. She was more tired than she realized and saw no harm in closing her eyes for a moment . . .

Stephen crested the trail and drew a deep breath of the clean, fragrant mountain air. He gazed down at Ella, sleeping in his arms, and had to resist the urge to kiss her for fear of waking her. He took a few more steps, letting the mountain flowers and ferns brush his pant legs. Then he became aware that an Amish woman stood a small distance from him, and when she turned, he drew a sharp intake of breath.

"Mamm," he acknowledged.

"What is this?" His mother's green eyes swept darkly over Ella.

"Everything that matters," he returned, and realized that he spoke the truth . . .

Ella rubbed her eyes with the back of her hand and became aware that Stephen was speaking—low, level, yet somehow angry. She looked up at him and realized that they were in a clearing with high pine trees surrounding them.

A shrill female voice broke Ella's appreciation of the trees, and she stiffened in Stephen's arms.

"You dare to return here with a woman in your arms— an *Englisch* woman?" The words were provoking.

Against her will, thoughts of her uncle's cruel voice surfaced, and Ella struggled to get down and face this accuser.

Stephen lowered her slowly, solicitously, but kept his arms about her waist and placed a firm hand on her belly. "*Jah*—an *Englisch* girl. And we *kumme* bearing gifts— she's *ime familye weg*."

"Pregnant?" The older woman's voice rose an octave. "You married an *Englischer*?"

"Did I say we were married?" Stephen drawled softly. Ella wasn't sure who was more shocked—herself, or the shrewish little woman dressed in Amish black. *And yet, he's told no lie—just insinuated* . . . But still, if the woman before her was representative of the community at large, it was no wonder Stephen didn't especially like the place.

Ella laced her hands over Stephen's against her belly. She was unsure of exactly what to say but knew she longed to defend Stephen somehow from this stranger.

"You bring us shame," the woman accused.

Ella felt rather than saw Stephen's stiff half bow.

"Shame . . . as always," he said clearly. "Ella, meet my mother."

Viola Lambert entered her mountain home with a heavy heart. Her sister, Esther, looked up from some darning she was doing and gave her a sharp glance.

"What is it, Vi?"

"Stephen is *heiser*. I saw him by the tall trees. He has a pregnant *Englisch* woman with him." Viola felt some relief in saying the words, but still, her heart pounded with the idea that he wasn't married.

Esther put aside her sewing and Viola felt the weight of her stare. Always Esther, the older, the wiser, had given Viola direction in life—even when Viola had married and borne Stephen. And then, when Ben was killed in a hunting accident, Esther had told Viola that it was the will of *Derr Herr* and that she'd never approved of Ben in the first place.

Viola drew herself away from such thoughts and carefully put her herb basket on the kitchen table. She was ready for the next question but did not know how to answer.

"Pregnant?" Esther snapped. "So he married an *Englischer*? Well, knowing the bishop, he'll welcome the two back to Ice Mountain with open arms."

"They're not married." *There. It's out.* Viola fingered the handle of the woven basket and looked away from Esther, but her older sister's words still cut deep.

"First an accused murderer and now a fornicator— Well, Viola, I'd say he's like his father and you can expect nothing more from him. Shun him, I say."

Viola's throat grew tight. "Haven't I shunned him already?"

Stephen was all too familiar with the mocking guise he kept up around his *mamm* and *aenti*—it was much safer than allowing any room for their barbs. He supposed it was childish in a way, to coldly close up instead of facing the women head-on, but he knew no other way to keep the pain from cutting deep.

"Stephen? Are you all right?"

He looked up and smiled at Ella's soft question. They were sitting in a small field of spring wildflowers because it was a place he'd often run after a scolding from his mother and *aenti*. Now it seemed like an opportune time to show Ella some of his favorite spots on the mountain.

"I'm as right as I can be, given our welcome an hour ago."

"You let her think the baby was ours—I mean, yours— you know what I mean."

He reached out and covered her thin fingers with his hand, not wanting to see her flustered. "I did, Ella, but if you want me to undo it, I will."

"Are you ashamed of me?"

"What?" he exclaimed, dropping the daisy stem he'd been toying with as he moved closer to put an arm around her shoulders.

"Well," she said, exhaling softly, "it would make a lot of sense. I'm pregnant, unmarried . . . your people are innocent, guided by their Old Order faith and—"

"My people are just like any other people," he said drily. "Some good, some bad, and a whole lot in between. And *nee*, I'm not ashamed of you. I just instinctively claimed the babe as mine—not for any other reason,

Ella, than perhaps I wish it were so. That the baby is mine—ours."

"And the unmarried part?" She arched a dark eyebrow, and he laughed. He couldn't help it—it seemed as though a whole color spectrum of emotion was open to him when he was with her, and he easily dropped a kiss on her mouth.

"The unmarried part—well, *jah*, to irritate Mamm, but I didn't want to claim something that you might not want."

"Oh," she whispered, turning to put her hands on his chest. "I might want . . ."

He heard the soft note of desire in her voice, and it flared through his senses like flame to a powder keg.

He kissed her without reservation, trying to drink her in as his fingers played through her long hair. He laid her down gently in the sweet-smelling grass, then cuddled beside her, slanting his head to deepen the kiss.

"Ahem!"

Stephen eased up, annoyed to be interrupted from such pleasure on a fine spring morning.

"I hope I'm not bothering you."

Stephen smiled when he saw who had spoken, and he helped Ella to her feet with quick tenderness, then reached out to pull his old friend into a hearty hug.

Ella watched as the two men embraced like brothers. She studied the lean, black-haired stranger and then felt like she wanted to turn away when his keen blue eyes swept over her. But he reached out an easy hand and spoke with gentleness.

"I'm Joel Umble. I hope Stephen might have said that he has some *gut* friends on Ice Mountain."

Ella decided she liked his smile and made a brief half

curtsy in response. "He might have mentioned one or two—especially the local bishop."

"Well then, will you both do me the pleasure of coming home to my family? I know you and my *frau* will have much to discuss, as she's expecting a baby about the same time as you are."

Ella blinked in surprise and looked to Stephen, who shrugged with a grin.

"Joel knows things, sort of like Lester does."

Ella smiled. "Then we will be in good company."

Stephen nodded. "*Jah*, Joel and Martha have many family members living with them, and they are all wonderful people. Joel's mother- and father-in-law as well as his great-grandmother by marriage are all invalids . . ."

"But that doesn't stop them from causing trouble," Joel joked. "Especially now that they can get more sun in their wheelchairs."

"How is your *mamm*?" Stephen asked his friend as Ella listened.

"Freed—is the only word I can use . . ." Joel smiled. "But *kumme*, we'll go home and have some coffee cake— it's Martha's specialty."

Ella nodded, glad for the chance to meet more of the mountain people.

Chapter Fourteen

Stephen wondered when the question would arise, and he didn't have long to wait. He'd left Ella and Joel's wife, Martha, busily chatting, while he and Joel went out to walk the grounds where the sheep were kept.

"It's not your child?" Joel asked softly as the sound of the creek bubbled pleasantly in the background.

Stephen looked into his friend's keen eyes and shook his head. "*Nee*."

"But you want it to be . . . And you're willing to risk everyone thinking you're just a negligent rogue who won't marry even when he should—it's sort of the same thing you did with the murder—letting everyone think what they might." Joel's voice was calm, knowing, and Stephen understood that his friend wasn't digging, but rather was being supportive.

Stephen shrugged. "So it's what I do."

"Ella seems like a nice *maedel*," Joel said cheerily, and Stephen rolled his eyes.

"She is, but let's cut to the chase, all right?" He

knocked shoulders with Joel and his friend came back at him with a laugh.

"*Ach*, in one way, it feels so good to be here," Stephen said, smiling. "But definitely not in another. Do you know we met my *mamm* when we first arrived?"

"Are you forgetting the Amish grapevine?"

"*Jah*, I suppose."

"I knew you were on Ice Mountain within ten minutes."

"Ha! You knew when I was carrying Ella up the trail." Stephen spoke lightly.

"You love her, don't you?"

Stephen stopped, his friend's words ricocheting off his heart. "*Jah*," he said finally. "For all that I know what love means—*jah*, I love her."

Ella gazed out at the beautiful kitchen garden that Martha Umble had invited her to see.

"Perhaps Stephen has told you that for our Amish 'there is no beauty without purpose,' so our gardens are not created just to be pretty. Rather, we gain peace once the work has been done."

"That's a wonderful thought, Martha." Ella smiled, glancing at the delightful young woman beside her. "When I was younger, I loved to paint the sea, but here you paint with your flowers and plants."

"I suppose that's true." Martha put her hand to her belly as if contemplating something, and Ella recognized the expression.

"Does your baby kick often?" Ella asked.

Martha laughed. "*Jah*, and it is still a wonder of *Gott* to me."

"Oh, I've never thought of that, but I suppose you are right."

"You don't sound so sure, maybe?" Martha asked shyly.

Ella shook her head. "About God? No—I haven't been, though I heard a good message about faith when we were in Coudersport."

Martha nodded her *kapp*ed head. "The Bible says that *Gott* knits us together in our mother's womb."

"I've never read that." Ella placed a hand on her own belly, then reached an impulsive hand out to Martha, who took it graciously.

"Friends?" Martha asked with a smile.

"Oh, yes," Ella answered, seeing serenity in the other woman's eyes. "Friends."

Stephen knew it would have been all too easy to stay with Joel and his family. Joel, as the new bishop, would have been a place of refuge for him and Ella. But Stephen also wanted to protect Ella from anyone searching for her, and hiding her at his reclusive *mamm*'s *haus* might be the best way to do that. But it would not be easy for him . . .

"Do you want me to carry you?" he asked softly when he felt her steps lag.

"No, I'm fine. I was only thinking that if there was a hotel here, it might be a little less awkward—than staying with your family and all."

He laughed then as she did about the hotel joke and pulled her close as they came out of the woods to a fair-sized clearing. "This is where my *mamm* and *aenti* live," he said, his voice level.

He felt Ella clutch his hand reassuringly. "It'll be all right, Stephen. You will see."

Stephen bent and swiped her mouth with a gentle kiss, then led her to the cabin.

Viola Lambert went to answer the firm knock on her door and resolutely undid the latch. She stared into the gloaming at her tall *sohn* and the *maedel* holding his hand.

"*Kumme* in," she said finally.

"*Danki*, Mamm," Stephen answered, and she nodded, clearing her throat a bit.

"Esther is lying down with a headache. I—I want to say—*ach*, what is your name?" she asked, looking at the other woman.

"I'm Ella Nichols—thank you for letting us stay with you." Viola froze when the girl bent forward and embraced her.

It felt foreign, odd, and somewhere—deep inside—touched a heart that had long been cold. *Certainly Stephen has not embraced me, but what reason have I given him to do so?* Viola realized that they were staring at her as she stood thinking, and she swallowed hard.

"Ella, you look tired. *Sei se gut kumme* to the table and I will give you something to eat and drink." She turned, then remembered with startling clarity—she hadn't invited her *sohn* to eat. She turned back to him and looked up into his beautiful eyes—his *fater*'s eyes. "Stephen, will you *kumme* to eat as well?"

Stephen stared down at his *mamm*, unsure of how to respond, but then he nodded and went to slide onto the simple bench at the table next to Ella. *When was the last time I was asked to come to the table?* Normally, before

he had been shunned from the community for being
accused of murder, Stephen had too often been seated at
a hated side table as punishment for whatever infraction
he'd committed: coming in late, breaking a neighbor's
window with a volleyball—all typical teenage stuff . . .
But his isolation had hurt, and he supposed that was what
the two women had been trying to accomplish.

Now he held Ella's hand under the main table and
waited as his mother brought fresh bread, crocks of butter
and preserves, raw milk, and a blueberry buckle to the
table. His *mamm* was a *gut* cook, and he noticed that Ella
didn't waste time before complimenting his mother.

"Oh, Mrs. Lambert—what good things you make! I
guess I'm more hungry now with the ba—" She trailed
off, and Stephen cleared his throat.

"Mamm—there's something we have to tell you, and
the fewer people on the mountain who know it, the better.
I think maybe you might not even tell Aenti Esther, but
you will have to decide. Mamm, Ella's life is in danger.
Her *onkel* and *aenti* want to kill her. We don't know why,
but I risked bringing her here to keep her safe. I told
Joel—I mean, the bishop earlier today, and he agreed to
let her stay and thought maybe since your cabin is a bit
remote, that it might be the right place for her to hide."

Stephen watched and waited as his *mamm* carefully
buttered a piece of bread; then she looked up. "Ella Nichols
may stay, but there is only one spare room. Where will you
sleep?"

Stephen met Ella's worried glance and shook his head
slightly. "It's all right. I will sleep in the room with her,
the better to guard and watch over her."

His mother arched a dark eyebrow. "It is what I would
expect you'd do . . . I will give you extra quilts so that you
may sleep on the floor, Stephen."

He almost had to laugh, amazed that his *mamm* had consented without an argument . . . It was strange how different she seemed, but he was sadly sure her old self would surface sooner or later. Still, he might enjoy the moment while it was here . . .

Ella knew he was watching her, and she shivered in the warmth of his blue-green gaze. He was lying on the floor, his shirt off, as he leaned his head up on one elbow. A bunch of quilts were tangled around his waist, and as Ella turned to comb through a difficult tendril, he suddenly got to his feet.

"Let me help you," he said hoarsely.

She nodded, not knowing what to expect. But then he climbed on the bed behind her and pulled her back between his bent knees. She shivered again in her thin white nightgown as the warmth of his wool-clad thighs penetrated through to her hips.

He took the comb from her with gentle fingers, then deftly began to work it through her hair.

Ella looked into the mirror above the dresser and saw them illuminated by kerosene lamplight. Stephen looked beautiful, his tan skin making hers appear all the more pale. Ella savored the lean line of his rib cage and the curve of his hip. His suspenders were down, and she watched the fascinating line of white skin near his waist as he arched to better get at the front of her hair. She longed to touch him there, along that stretch of white, where his tan didn't extend; her fingers curled in her lap and she dropped her gaze from the mirror.

She'd never really seen Jeremy's body—it had all been a rush, a rustling removal of clothes, more groping and far less intimate than the act Stephen was performing now for her. She cleared her throat.

"I didn't know men could do this," she murmured.

He put his hands gently on her shoulders and peered around to face her so that she was eye level with his mouth. "Do what?" he asked.

She wet her lips and thought about kissing him. "Hair . . . you know."

He smiled, and she smiled back in easy reaction.

"*Ach*, I can do a lot of things that might surprise you, Ella Nichols."

She felt herself flush and then he kissed her on the nose, leaving her feeling both flustered and confused.

He moved behind her again and returned to his combing, and Ella relaxed slowly under his careful hands, dreamily wondering if this was how he would make love . . .

He was making love to her, assuaging his frantic hunger with deep movements that cost him his breath and made his blood throb. Her breathy cries raked the periphery of his senses and he rolled to his back so that he might prolong their pleasure. But she moved atop him; subtle, confident— tightening so that he arched his back and barely swallowed the scream that came from low in his throat.

Stephen jerked upright, gasping, and felt the *nacht* breeze from the screened window cross his sweat-soaked skin. He looked over to see Ella sleeping peacefully on the bed and he lay back down in slow degrees, feeling that his fantasies and dreams about her were getting out of hand . . .

Chapter Fifteen

Ella lay in the bed and listened to the rain on the cabin roof. Stephen had obviously left the room before she awoke, as his quilts were folded neatly on a ladder-back chair. She wondered what exactly to do, feeling her stomach rumble when the bedroom door was eased open. Stephen entered, carrying a tray, and she sat up in bed, feeling suddenly hungry.

"Oh, thank you," she murmured, smiling at him. "I was about to come looking for food."

"*Gut*. It means the baby is healthy, I would imagine." He gently settled the tray on her lap, then sat down on the edge of the bed.

She studied his handsome profile for a moment. "What's wrong?"

He shook his dark head. "Nothing. Eat your toast."

She reached out and touched his hand, lacing her fingers through his. "Stephen, I know you—I think . . . I trust you. Please, what's wrong?"

He looked up at her, his beautiful eyes blue-green and earnest. "I hate to ask you, but it would make sense . . . Would you mind dressing as an Amish woman does? It would allow you to blend in with the community—the better to hide your existence here. Joel stopped by with a few of Martha's things that you might use."

"Of course I will, Stephen." She sat back and took a bite of buttered toast, feeling glad that she could ease his mind. Then she gave him a saucy smile. "You'll have to show me how to put them on correctly, you know."

His answering grin was wolfish, and her toes curled in pleasure beneath the mound of quilts.

"I'd be glad to be of service—and I think, Ella Nichols, that you're flirting with me."

She wanted to look away from his warm smile but couldn't as she finished off the toast.

A brusque knock on the door interrupted their word-play, and Ella nearly jostled the tray. Stephen rose and opened the latch; then Ella saw his long back straighten. She had thought it was his mother, but she didn't recognize the voice spouting a torrent of angry Penn Dutch from outside the room. Then Stephen closed the door abruptly and turned back to the bed.

"My *aenti* Esther at her most pleasant," he muttered, and Ella saw the tenseness around his mouth.

"Is that your mother's sister?"

"*Jah*," he sighed, reaching a hand to rub the back of his neck.

Ella thought for a quick moment. "Stephen—your mother was quite kind to me last night; perhaps your aunt needs some kindness herself—I mean—not from you, but I can—"

"You don't have to do anything, Ella. I won't have you stressed by trying to deal with her bitterness—it might hurt the baby. We're leaving this morning."

"Leaving? But I thought you said it was safe here."

Against her will, her voice quavered, and he came to kneel beside the bed.

"It is safe on Ice Mountain, but I know a better place where we can stay that is even farther back in the woods."

"A cave?" she questioned dubiously, and he laughed, his good humor visibly renewed.

"*Nee*, sweetheart. A cabin. It belonged—to a friend of mine. He's gone now, but he would have wished us to stay there. I'll get Joel and *geh* and fix anything that's in disrepair, and you can visit a friend of ours, May Miller—she's the healer on the mountain."

"All right," Ella agreed, still doubtful.

Then he lifted the tray from her lap and leaned forward to kiss her, and her world calmed into perspective. She trusted him to keep her safe . . .

Viola Lambert tried to let her sister's spiteful words fall away like the rain did from the slanted roof of the cabin. *But the rain brings new growth and nourishment, while my sister's words only make my bones feel brittle . . .* She swallowed a sigh and looked once more to the bedroom door where her *sohn* and Ella Nichols were staying. Esther must have tracked Viola's gaze, because she put the teakettle down with a loud thump.

"And what are they doing in there? Fornicating, no doubt, while we wait outside and give them privacy for their lusts."

"They had a long hike up the mountain yesterday—perhaps they—she still needs rest." Viola's voice shook a bit in this rare contradiction of Esther and she sought to steady it. "I hope *es bobbel* is well."

"Bah—pregnant and unwed—what wellness could there be for a baby in this? Viola, you are growing soft

just because your addlepated *sohn* chose to *kumme* back
to your home . . . The *buwe* is as worthless as his *fater*
was, and you know—"

Suddenly, Esther's words faded as Viola was struck by
a distinct memory of Stephen's *fater*, Ben. *My husband.*
My lover—who would freely kiss me no matter who was
about . . . She put a hand up to touch her cold lips with
tentative fingers, then nearly jumped as Stephen opened
the bedroom door and came into the kitchen with a beautiful woman dressed in Amish clothing behind him . . .

"Mamm . . . Aenti Esther . . . doesn't Ella look well in
Amish dress?" Stephen asked, keeping his voice low.
"Ella, meet my *aenti* Esther, by the way." He automatically stepped in front of Ella, wanting no malevolence
from his *aenti* to touch her or the babe.

Before Ella or Esther could speak, Stephen addressed
his mother. "Mamm, after consideration, we thank you
for the room, but I fear Ella must have an even more
remote place to rest in safety. I'm going up the mountain
to—Dan's—to my *auld* cabin."

He ignored the strangely stricken look on his *mamm's*
face and took Ella by the hand. "The rain has slowed.
We'll head out now."

"Thank you for breakfast, and it was—nice—to meet
you, Aenti Esther." Ella spoke quietly, but his *aenti* remained
cold and silent, as did his *mamm*.

Stephen exhaled once they were free of the heavy
atmosphere of the cabin.

He took a few steps, his arm around Ella, and stopped
to listen to the soft raindrops pattering on the canopy of
leaves overhead. Even if he hadn't asked for *Gott's* blessing, he felt renewed in his spirit by the touch of *Gott's*

Hand on the place, and he began to walk with Ella, pausing now and then to consider why he felt so satisfied seeing her in Amish dress.

"What is it?" she asked. "Do I look strange?" She put a hesitant hand to the *kapp* on her neatly coiled red hair.

"*Nee*, you look—nice."

"Nice?" She frowned. "I guess that's good."

He smiled and shook his head. *How can I tell her that she's the most enticing thing I've ever seen?* He let his gaze roam over her in the Amish dress of blue that she wore with its white apron. He had intimate knowledge of where each straight pin was placed against her fair skin, even though he'd only given verbal directions as to the dressing, not trusting himself to touch her. Now, as the rain picked up a bit, he stopped and nestled her close, wanting to feel the baby kick again and to drink Ella in like fine blackberry wine during a summer's moist heat.

But then she shivered. He realized he was risking her health by keeping her out in the wet weather, and he caught her right hand in a firm grip. They ran, laughing and breathless, through the wooded paths to May Miller's cabin, but no one answered his knock.

"*Kumme*," he shouted over what had become a downpour. "The healer's cabin is always unlatched."

He tugged the handle and they both practically fell inside as the storm became a subdued roar. Stephen listened to Ella working for breath, and without preamble, he began to pull pins from her wet clothes.

"Stephen!" She gasped as her apron fell away. "What are you doing?"

"Undressing you." He slid another pin from its place. "I'm not looking. I just want you dry."

Ella giggled, her teeth chattering, then stepped lightly

away from him when he tried to slip her dress over her head. "I can manage. Suppose the healer lady comes back?"

"She'll agree with me that you should be dry and warm."

She curtsied in front of him. "Very well. But what about you? You're wet too." She stepped toward him quickly and tugged one suspender down.

He was amazed at how fast the mood changed for him; desire flared through him at her playfulness, and he took a step closer to her. "Yes, I am wet outside, but inside, I'm suddenly very hot."

She met his gaze and he saw an answering heat in her dark eyes that turned him upside down. He caught her next to him and shivered as her slender fingers teased his other suspender off his shoulder . . .

Chapter Sixteen

Ella loved the moment when his thick lashes lowered, shielding his sea-colored eyes. She knew then that he was deep in the act of kissing her, not concentrating on anything else. She returned his kisses with innocent fervor, even running the tip of her tongue across his lips. But she was unprepared for the reaction her subtle gesture produced in him.

"*Ach*, Ella," he groaned. "*Sei se gut*—I want—" He broke off his words to snatch ruthlessly at his shirt, and she heard the faint sound of pins hitting the hardwood floor. She wanted to help him, but he'd already thrust the fabric off his body, and she reveled in the sight of his bare chest. It was then that she noticed he was bleeding from a thin scratch near his lean ribs.

"Stephen, one of the pins scratched you."

"I don't care," he muttered, and she had to smile as he bent to claim her lips once more. Then some instinctive response came to her and she pulled from him slightly to bend and lick at the brief scratch on his tan skin. She felt him shudder and delighted in the power she knew at that moment to arouse him.

His movements grew frantic, and she yielded gladly as he nudged her up to the kitchen table. She thought she might soon feel the hard oak beneath her back and was breathless at the notion, but he turned suddenly, gracefully, and then she was atop him on the table. She placed her hands on his shoulders for balance and bent to begin kissing him once more.

She soon lifted her head though when she realized that the cabin door latch had clicked and was quickly opened. Ella stared into the eyes of the other woman with fascinated embarrassment.

"Well, Stephen Lambert." The woman smiled briefly. "You make an interesting centerpiece, but I must ask you politely to dress."

Ella was surprised to feel Stephen's broad shoulders shake with laughter as he sat up and caught her close. "My apologies, May. Please meet Ella Nichols."

There was no way Ella could imagine scrambling off the table, so she smiled lamely and gave her greetings instead.

"One *nacht*?" Joel asked in faint exasperation, and Stephen shrugged. The two friends were up in the high timber, at old Dan's abandoned cabin, making minor repairs to the relatively snug little place. The sound of the rain pattering on the carpet of leaves beneath his feet was soothing to Stephen, and he enjoyed the occasional breaks of companionable silence between himself and Joel as they checked the foundation.

"I'll not have Ella and the baby subjected to those women's negativity. I know you told me to stay there,

Joel, with my *mamm* and *aenti*, but one *nacht* was about all I could handle."

"So how did you and Ella meet?" Joel's tone was casual as he changed the subject, and Stephen shrugged.

"She was in a fire. I helped her out."

"Why do I think there is a little bit more to the story?"

Stephen half smiled. "I'm a fireman. It's what I do."

"You're also part of this Amish community. Do you plan on staying for any length of time? We could always use someone familiar with fire on Ice Mountain."

"I don't know, Joel. I'll stay as long as it keeps Ella safe." He knelt to inspect a small hole in the foundation and pulled together the materials to fix it.

Stephen got down on his knees, and Joel leaned against the side of the cabin.

"What do you say we take a break after this before we clean the inside of the cabin?"

"So you can preach to me?" Stephen smiled ruefully up at his friend.

"I *am* the bishop hereabouts."

"How could I forget? All right, I'll take the preaching, but we'll sweeten the deal with me getting the lion's share of your wife's strawberry pie from that lunch you brought."

"Done!" Joel pledged and Stephen sighed aloud.

Ella had resumed most of her composure as she sat down to tea with the healer of Ice Mountain, May Miller. Ella averted her gaze from the kitchen table and concentrated instead on the naturally sweet rose tea her hostess had served her.

"The tea is lovely, thank you. And I—I'm sorry for

my—our—behavior earlier." Ella once more looked away from the hickory plank table.

"You're impulsive, but I'm sure Stephen can be—compelling," May said quietly, and Ella nodded. It was difficult to disagree with this other woman, who appeared young but had wise old dark eyes. *And I am impulsive, which is why I'm pregnant . . .*

"There is no room for shame when you are going to bring a new life into the world." May smiled as she sipped her tea.

Ella blinked back sudden tears as she once more felt that she was understood on some deep level by a person she barely knew. She shrugged uncomfortably. "I know—I guess. Sometimes I wonder what my father would say . . ."

"Your *Fater* in heaven created this life in your womb."

"I haven't thought about that much." Ella felt her spirits lift. "It is amazing to think that God would be so gracious to me—I'm the least likely person to know Him very well."

"Grace is a gift from *Derr Herr*—free to all."

"Yes. I'll have to remember that." Ella felt a sense of peace come over her, and she became suddenly quite drowsy.

May rose from the table and took her hand. "*Kumme.* Carrying the babe makes you tired. You can nap in my bed."

"Oh, I couldn't," Ella said with a yawn, but then conceded. "Well, maybe for few minutes."

The healer led her into the next room, and soon Ella was slipping into a pleasant lassitude in the folds of a soft featherbed, barely noticing when May drew the quilts over her.

* * *

The bark and moss were damp on the surface of the large fallen tree that made a perfect seat to eat lunch and talk. Stephen, as promised, was offered a larger piece of Martha's sweet strawberry pie, but he shared evenly just the same. He enjoyed the hearty ham sandwiches on homemade bread with their sharp bite of ground horse-radish and the sweet macaroni and potato salad portions. He wondered what Ella was doing back in the healer's cabin, then suppressed the thought when he caught Joel's eye.

"I miss Martha during the day too," the bishop pointed out.

Stephen rolled his eyes. "You were going to preach to me, remember? Not talk about women."

"Right . . . So, this coming Sunday is church meeting. I'd like both you and Ella to be there—if she's feeling up to it. I've decided that the best thing we can do to protect her is to tell the whole story to the community after the service."

"You're probably right, but uh, you forget, my friend, that there are probably those who would prefer to see me shunned for leaving the mountain to firefight. It—will be hard to get up in front of everybody."

Joel nodded slowly. "*Jah*, but just say the truth that's on your heart, and all will be well."

"Well, I doubt it, but I'll try."

"Sounds *gut* to me!" Joel slapped his right knee.

But Stephen gave his friend a sour smile and did not share in his enthusiasm.

Viola Lambert opened the heavy chest, and the smell of mothballs and cedar rose up to fill her nostrils. She was alone; Esther had gone to swap quilt squares with a distant neighbor. And, for some reason, Viola knew a keen sadness in the quiet of the cabin and had been drawn to Ben's trunk. Of course, she reflected, Esther had urged her to give away all of Ben's things, as was only charitable . . . but there were a few items she had kept in secret from her older sister.

Now she laid aside a stack of patchwork quilts and reached to the very bottom of the chest. She felt for the tissue paper, and then her fingers touched the light cotton material. She felt her heart beat a bit faster as she pulled out the shirt. Instinctively, she pressed it to her face and took a deep breath. Past the smell of cedar and age, she knew there was the scent of Ben—pine and salt, winter sunshine and spring rain. Against her will, she felt her eyes fill with tears. *How proud and happy Ben felt when Stephen was born, and how joyful I was at Ben's pleasure . . . But then came the hunting accident—just before Stephen turned six months old—and Esther moved in . . . to help, to help, but* ach, *how she hurt me sometimes . . . me and Stephen.*

Viola swallowed hard and resolutely put the shirt back in its place. What *gut* was it to think uncharitable thoughts about her older sister? Esther was undoubtedly right—most of the time. *And surely, surely what Esther says about the depravity of Stephen and Ella Nichols must be true* . . . She placed the quilts back hastily and got to her feet, remembering that she had promised to go to Sol Kauffman's for baking powder. She hoped the brisk walk would clear her mind—and heart.

Ella was in the languorous place between waking and sleep when she felt the hot press of lips against her throat. She forgot that she was in the healer's bed and stretched deliciously. "Mmmm," she murmured, smiling, delighting in the sensation. She arched her back and turned her head on the thick pillow, wanting the kisses to go on and on. She'd never felt this way with Jeremy, and she sensed on an instinctual level that it was Stephen who kissed her— heated, handsome Stephen, who could wipe away all rational thought from her mind. She felt their tongues meet in a sultry dance—wet, insistent, and she knew a burning deep inside. She wanted something but didn't know what it was. "Please," she whispered, half opening her eyes even as she felt him pull back slightly.

Please? Please what? Stephen drew in a ragged breath. *Am I to touch her here, in May Miller's bed?* He felt the idea was not without merit, but then his conscience suddenly intruded; a reserved Amish conscience that surprised him . . . *I am not married to Ella. She has no one to protect her or the baby, and I promised to be her friend.* It was like a bucket of icy water being poured down his back, and he withdrew from her arms despite the sound of protest that came, sultry and high, from the back of her delicate throat.

"Don't take umbrage with me! I had no part in the fool turning himself in." Douglas Nichols growled the words low, but his wife looked unconcerned.

"Douglas, what are you worried about? A letter from Mitch Wagner talking twaddle about the Light?" She moved toward him with a serpentine swing of her hips. "Besides, darling, I've found someone much—colder— in nature. He'll take care of any potential talk and investigation Wagner's babble may produce, and we will own the Sea Glass Castle free and clear of our dear redheaded niece."

"Humph! Well, who have you found? I admit my man has not panned out, and your instincts are usually right."

"Thank you, darling. I'll have him sent in . . . His name is Jeremy Collier."

Chapter Seventeen

"I'd like us to stop by Sol Kauffman's store to get a few supplies before we head up to the cabin." Stephen was infinitely grateful to be back on safe footing with Ella—anything had to be better than the torturous feelings he'd known when kissing her in May's bed.

He glanced down at her now, walking beside him in the still-wet day, and took her hand lightly. She slid her fingers through his with all the trust of a child and he once again had to tell himself that it was going to be all right living alone with her at the cabin—despite the obvious temptation. The key, he considered, as he indicated the dirt path to the store, would be to hang on to the thought that he was her friend and protector. If he could do that, all should be well. He was actually surprised that Joel had allowed their living situation; but Joel was Joel, and the mountain would know the truth soon enough.

"You're deep in thought."

Her soft voice roused him and he smiled at her. "I'm sorry. I wanted to tell you that Joel invited us to church this coming Sunday."

He saw her dubious glance and squeezed her hand.

"Will I be welcome?" she asked, and he didn't miss that she pressed her free hand to her belly.

"*Jah*—you both will be welcome. I will introduce you and tell the community your story—our story. Then, likely they will make known to us that you are safe here."

She nodded, and he longed to wipe the concern from her brow, but they had reached the store, and he led her up the stairs with a gentle hand.

Sol Kauffman's general store had anything and everything within its humble confines, and it was always stimulating to one's senses to enter the place. Today was no different, and Stephen drew in a quick, appreciative breath redolent with peppermint candy, cooking spices, leather, and sharp cheese.

"Oh, my," Ella whispered to him.

"What is it?"

"I feel like I could eat everything in here."

They laughed softly together, and he would have taken a quick moment to swipe a kiss across her nose if a cutting female voice hadn't interrupted from the aisle in front of him.

Ruby Raber was a girl who'd been sweet on him over the past few years, and he stifled a groan at meeting her with Ella on his arm. Ruby no doubt felt a certain proprietorship over him, even though he'd never even hinted at courting with her. He wanted to explain all of this to Ella but didn't have time as Ruby stepped close and spoke bitingly.

"Stephen Lambert—I'd heard you'd left Ice Mountain for the *Englisch* world." Ruby's gaze raked Ella. "Or did you bring part of the *Englisch* back with you—no matter her dress—or condition?"

Stephen smiled grimly as he felt Ella tense up against him.

"Ruby—this is Ella Nichols. Ella, this is Ruby Raber—a friend." He said this last word slowly, wondering if Ruby had ever truly been his friend, as Ella seemed to be.

But then, Sol Kauffman called out to them from behind his counter and Stephen excused himself and drew Ella from Ruby's path.

"Hiya! Hiya there, Stephen!" The store owner was a bear of a man, both tall and rotund. Sol was always full of news and good cheer, and he came around the corner to welcome Ella with a giant handshake and the presentation of the licorice jar. "Take one, my *maedel*!" Stephen caught a glimpse of Ella's smile and a surge of pleasure filled his heart to see her so welcomed.

"Sol only hands round the candy jar when he's really happy," Stephen confided in Ella's ear.

She nodded and graciously curtsied to the big man, whose face reddened at her gesture.

"*Kumme* now," Sol blustered. "What else can I get for you folks, huh?"

"We've got quite a list." Stephen produced a crumpled paper from his pocket and handed it over, while he watched Ella slowly wander away from him toward the cracker barrel, then teeter suddenly.

He quickly followed and caught her wrist in his hand, feeling her frantic pulse beat. One look at her pale face told him all he needed to know. He scooped her up against his chest and spoke in hurried tones to Sol. "Ella's feeling faint—I'll take her out for some fresh air."

Sol waved away his words. "*Nee*, Stephen, bring her into the back. Frau Loftus will make some tea for her and she can rest on the couch."

Stephen obeyed the older man and stepped around the counter through a long curtain that Sol held aside. Then Sol followed his friend into the back of the store, which was Sol's family home. Stephen nodded at Frau Loftus as she turned with a baby on her hip and a toddler hiding in her skirts; then he carefully lowered Ella to the comfortable-looking couch that Sol indicated.

Ella looked up at him and smiled despite her pallor. "I'm fine, Stephen."

"I know," he whispered. "But just lie still for a few minutes."

Frau Loftus bustled over with a teacup and saucer. "*Ach*, poor *maedel*! The pregnancy is not easy sometimes, hmmm?"

Stephen watched Ella accept the warm tea and wondered vaguely if everyone on Ice Mountain already knew about Ella and the baby.

Viola straightened her bonnet and walked up the steps of Sol Kauffman's store. She liked to get her shopping done and leave the place, not wanting to socialize—but today, Ruby Raber flounced into her path as soon as she entered.

"Frau Lambert, *gut* day. I had the questionable pleasure of seeing Stephen and his—*Englischer* inside. And of course," Ruby continued, her voice becoming saccharine sweet, "she had to feign passing out so he had to carry her—and—and . . . Well, never mind. I hope I don't have to lay eyes on either of them again!"

Viola drew in a sharp breath. Used to Esther's tirades, Viola found that this girl sounded like a purring kitten, and she almost told her so. Instead she merely nodded and continued on into the store.

Once inside, Viola moved hastily to the baking aisle and was pondering the merits of teaberry candy or peppermints for Esther's sweet tooth when Sol Kauffman came hurriedly toward her. It felt as if she was being cornered by a galloping rhinoceros and she was sure that everyone in the store heard the owner's booming words. "Right back here, Frau Lambert . . . Stephen's got the *maedel* lying down. You remember how light-headed you could become when you were carrying, I'd imagine . . . Just *kumme* with me."

Carrying? Carrying what? A rutabaga or an oversized grapefruit? But nee, *how about a* boppli, *a babe, how about Stephen himself. Can I remember what it felt like? Ben was so caring and tender . . . ach, how he loved me . . . But none of that matters now—he's gone . . .*

Sol swept her into the back of the store and through the curtain to the Kauffman home. Viola glanced over to where Stephen knelt beside Ella Nichols as she lay on the couch. She told herself that she didn't need to see the raw concern on her *sohn*'s face, that she didn't want to see it . . . Yet Sophia Loftus pulled a chair close to the couple and Viola sat down automatically even as one of the many Kauffman babies was plopped on her lap.

Sophia smiled down at her. "There. You must practice, Frau Lambert—the dandle on the knees . . . Besides, Ben is a happy baby."

Viola ignored the raised eyebrow of her *sohn* and tried to concentrate on the sweet-smelling baby in her lap. *If Esther could see me, she'd think I was an old fool—of course, Esther has no time for children.* The baby pulled at the front of her dress and she gently reached to rub his downy head. Images, soft and wondrous, played behind her eyes—holding Stephen close while Ben held them both near his heart, recognizing the cry and need of her *sohn* . . . My sohn, *my* boppli . . . Against her will, her eyes lifted to Stephen and Ella and she swallowed hard. The years since Ben had died seemed to have been swallowed up in fear and worry and anger—

"Mamm, you'll have to excuse us."

Stephen's deep voice and remote tone shook her from her thoughts. She watched him help Ella to her feet as the baby in her lap suddenly began to wail. Things hard and deep churned in Viola's chest as she automatically began to hum a disjointed tune. Stephen and Ella had already made their *gut*byes before Sophia Loftus came to take Ben from her lap. Viola left the store without the baking powder or the candy . . .

Chapter Eighteen

Ella had considered the interior of Stephen's mother's cabin to be sparse in decoration, as she knew was fitting for the plain people. But the cabin Stephen led her to in the high timber was a place of almost artistic charm.

Snowshoes, long-handled tools, and preserved pelts hung about the exposed beam walls. A rustic rock fireplace took up one wall, while a cookstove and bent willow bed occupied nearly the whole of the other side of the tiny home. There was just enough room for a small table and chairs and an old-fashioned rocker.

"It's charming," she said, smiling up at Stephen. Then she followed his gaze to the big bed. A quilt of pretty flower designs lay atop the mattress and two fluffy pillows looked comfortable at the head of the bed.

"*Jah*," he murmured. "Joel and Martha sent the bedding—but—I'll sleep on the floor."

Ella turned to face him. "Stephen . . . friends, remember? I think we can share the bed and there will be no—um—problems. Besides, I wouldn't feel right to have you on the floor!"

But she saw by the set of his jaw that his mind was

made up and she stopped trying to persuade him; instead she asked if he would like something to eat.

"Frau Loftus packed a bunch of different things for us in with the groceries you bought." Ella moved to the wicker basket Stephen had carried to the high timber and lifted the flat lid. She pulled out bags of sugar, flour, and brown sugar, as well as other various baking supplies. Then she uncorked a small brown bottle and breathed in the heavenly scent of vanilla.

She saw Stephen smile at the expression on her face and he came forward and took the bottle from her fingers. "Did you ever taste vanilla?" he asked softly.

"Mmm-hmmm. Our housekeeper told me not to but I ran outside in the sunshine with the bottle and took a big swallow. Ugh!" She made a face.

"Ah, but maybe you don't know the secret of tasting vanilla." His voice was low and she gazed up at him with suspicion, feeling the nerves in her belly begin to tauten and dance.

"What's the secret?" she asked, surprised when her voice came out as a high squeak.

"Well—" He rocked his hips closer to her so that his long legs pressed against her Amish dress. "You need to put something sweet behind the vanilla taste."

She furrowed her brow in confusion. "Wh—what do you mean?"

He reached his hand to gently ease his fingers beneath her *kapp*. "Sweet . . . like back here." He pulled his hand away and she watched rather breathlessly as he poured a drop of vanilla on his forefinger then moved to brush the wetness against her neck.

"Stephen . . . I . . ." She made a hoarse sound of pleasure when she felt his tongue follow the dampness on her skin. Then he was facing her again, and she bit her lip at the raw sensuality displayed in the depths of his now-green eyes . . .

Sweet . . . sweet . . . sweet . . . He continued to dab the vanilla on her cheek . . . her forehead . . . and then her red lips. He kissed her without reservation, his head in a tumult. He had no idea what he was doing—*except . . . That wasn't quite the truth . . .*

He wrenched himself away from her and smacked the vanilla bottle back on the table so hard that it would have tipped had Ella not caught it with what he realized were shaky hands.

He turned from her, his gaze riveted to a spot outside the nearest cabin window.

"I'm sorry," he muttered.

"You'll have to understand if I don't forgive you right away," she returned in what he considered to be a stormy tone.

"Don't cry, Ella . . . *sei se gut* . . . I couldn't bear it if you cried."

He felt her move beside him but he didn't take his eyes off the window. "Stephen? What's wrong?"

He shook his head, and he knew the moment her eyes followed his.

"Oh, there's a gravestone outside," Ella murmured. "Do you know whose it is?"

It took him a full half minute to answer. "Yeah—he was—a friend." The difficult words edged out from the back of his throat. He swallowed hard, trying to hold the memories at bay. But then he saw himself, holding the cold wooden handle of the shovel. Digging the grave as punishment for the crime . . .

"Stephen?" Ella touched his arm and he turned, swiping at his eyes.

"Stephen, you're crying." She stood suddenly on tiptoe and put her arms around him, holding him close. "I'm sorry that you miss your friend so much. Is that what's wrong?" Her words were gentle, tender, and he choked back a sob.

"His name was Dan Zook—he was murdered—shot in his own bed."

There was a long pause and then she sighed. "So, it was he who everyone thought you—"

"I let them think it," he bit out. "I suppose I wanted them to think it . . . My *mamm* and *aenti* had blamed me for one thing or another for as long as I could remember, so when the *auld* bishop pronounced me guilty of murder, I said nothing to defend myself."

"But Stephen, why did the bishop believe . . . ?"

"I'd been up here in the high timber and I came upon a pregnant doe—she'd been shot by a poacher. I could do nothing to save her but I had my knife and tried to help the fawn. I failed . . . I failed and I was covered in blood. Blood on a white shirt was enough to convince most of the community when the bishop had me stand before them. Everyone but Joel felt I was guilty. The bishop—he decided that I would be shunned, but first I would have to dig Dan's grave. This was Dan's cabin—it's where I lived until the truth became known about the actual murderer. We later found out that Joel Umble's older brother had killed Dan. After that, it was clear to everyone that I was innocent."

He heard her soft inhalation and wanted to muffle himself in the folds of her dress—to hide and cry out that he'd felt shunned all of his life. But Dan—Dan had been a true friend and father figure. His burial still shook Stephen . . . made him feel unclean somehow. But Ella's gentle touch was a balm for his senses and he slowly pulled himself together.

"*Danki*, Ella," he said, lifting his head.

"You're welcome." She stretched to kiss his cheek. "I understand now why you became a firefighter."

"Why's that?"

"Because you've spent your life in trials by fire and you're probably all the stronger because of them."

He smiled faintly. "*Gott* gives us strength—but I like knowing you understand part of me now."

She reached to give the vanilla bottle a faint tip and looked up at him rather wickedly. "I'd like to understand more of you," she murmured.

He pulled her close with alacrity. "Now that—would truly be . . . our pleasure."

Ella set out a generous meal for the two of them and found that she could barely hold Stephen's gaze across the food-laden table. *It's silly really,* she thought. Just a few vanilla kisses . . . But she knew her face was flushed with the memory of how the skin of his throat had tasted and how bold she'd become in finding a spot along his shoulder to kiss that had made him loosen his shirt with quick movements. But, she sighed to herself, then he had pulled away from her, apparently regaining control much faster than she.

Now he was looking at her with sea blue eyes as the quiet lengthened while they ate. Ella grew restive under the sound of silence.

"I can bake things," she burst out and he gave her a slow smile.

"Can you?" he asked with interest while he spread apple butter on a piece of Sophia Loftus's whole-grain bread.

She nodded, remembering the pristine kitchen at the Sea Glass Castle and the numerous baking lessons she'd had with their housekeeper, Mrs. Broom.

"I can indeed. Any kind of cookie you want."

He laughed. "*Ach, nee* . . . then I'm to be tempted at every turn?"

She raised an eyebrow at him, wondering if there was a double meaning in his casual words. "You'll be tempted no more than usual, sir. You simply must exercise restraint."

"Well . . ." He grinned at her. "There's the rub . . ."

Chapter Nineteen

Stephen listened to every rustle Ella made as she got situated in the big rope bed. His own bed, on the hard wood floor, was not nearly as comfortable, but it was far more conducive to his peace of mind. Ella was a constant temptation to him, and now, having shared what he had about Dan, he felt closer to her than ever.

"Are you awake?" Her soft voice seemed part of the *nacht*, and he thought about not answering.

"*Jah*."

"What are you thinking about?"

You . . . in my arms . . . "Not much . . . just listening to the crickets."

"They make a symphony all their own, don't they?" she asked.

"Mmm-hmmm."

"Stephen—I—oh!"

Her cry was one of pain and he jumped to his feet, feeling frantically for the kerosene lamp beside the bed.

"Is it the baby?" *Dear Gott, let it not be the baby!*

"N—no. My leg!" She was rubbing her calf muscle in

obvious desperation and he moved her hands away to massage the area himself.

"Charley horse," he muttered, trying to slow his heart rate. "We need to drink more water . . ."

She finally relaxed back against the pillows, and he sucked in a deep breath of air. "It's all right now, Stephen . . . but . . ."

"But what?" He ran his eyes over her, looking for any other problem.

"Stephen—you said 'we.' 'We have to drink more water . . .'"

"Right." He nodded. "It'll help with the leg cramping. But we should also check with May Miller tomorrow."

She smiled at him and he felt caught and held by her gaze. "Do you know how wonderful you are?" she asked softly.

He had no idea how to respond to her words. He knew that brushing them off would do her a disservice but no one had ever told him he was wonderful before and it was hard to take in.

"Maybe I'll believe that someday, Ella Nichols . . . maybe someday."

Jeremy Collier ran a self-assured hand through his blond hair and took a seat on the train headed out of Cape May. The fact that he was planning murder did little to disturb his peace of mind—in fact, the proposed victim herself was of little consequence in his thoughts. Ella Nichols might still be carrying the brat, and getting rid of her would eliminate more than one problem from his calculating mind. Of course, it had occurred to him that he might hold her for ransom and let her aunt and uncle pay to have her executed. But, after thinking it through, he knew he was somewhat of a coward and had no desire to get caught in the cross fire and end up dead himself.

He patted the breast pocket of his suit as he gazed at the slow-moving scenery outside the train window. Nichols's payment included a nice bonus if he could also rid the world of Mitch Wagner to eliminate any possible connection between himself and his niece.

Jeremy glanced up as a boy selling newspapers passed down the aisle; he bought one, then curled up comfortably behind its sheltering pages and, feeling bored, went to sleep.

In the first pink light of dawn, Ella awoke, momentarily confused as to where she was, but then she looked down to the floor and saw Stephen sprawled among a tangled pile of quilts. She studied him covertly, admiring the lean lines of his back and the strength of his shoulders. He was so beautiful and so hurt—she thought about all that he had shared with her the day before, and she knew that she was falling in love with him in a way that she had never cared for Jeremy. In fact, Jeremy seemed like some long-ago, unsettling dream, while Stephen made her smile and clearly cared for her and her baby. In fact, she felt a togetherness with Stephen that she had not experienced since she had been in her father's home.

Stephen stirred a bit, and she leaned back against the pillows, not wanting to be caught studying him. She wondered what it would be like to be an Amish housewife like Martha was to Joel. The other woman seemed to know such serenity, but Ella realized that peace did not come from putting on a *kapp* or pinning on a dress. No, based on what Pastor Rook had taught back in Coudersport, true peace could only come from God.

* * *

"Breakfast is ready, sweetheart."

Stephen sat on the edge of the bed and watched Ella wake and stretch with a tousled beauty that more than stirred his heart.

"Oh my, I'm sorry. I must have fallen back to sleep. I was up earlier." She gave a delicate yawn behind her hand.

He leaned forward and kissed her forehead. "You sleep because of the babe, but now *kumme* and have some food."

He helped her to her feet, then she folded back the sleeves of the overly large cotton nightgown that Frau Loftus had given her. She found that she was starving and was pleasantly surprised at the plate he set before her. Scrambled eggs, bacon, fresh grilled tomatoes, and toast did much to assuage her appetite.

"Thank you, Stephen," she said when they were through. "It's hard to believe, sitting here in this bright cabin, that my aunt and uncle want to kill me."

He shook his head and gave her a sober look. "It haunts me . . . I wonder—you said something to that Mitch Wagner about a letter and a will. Can you tell me what they have to do with your aunt and uncle?"

She smiled sadly. "There was a letter that my father left, and also his will, that named me his heir and legal owner of the Sea Glass Castle. My uncle had hidden them both, and he knew a lawyer who made sure he got title to the place. But one day I found both of them hidden in my uncle's study."

"What did you do next?"

He watched a myriad of emotions cross her pale face, and she placed a hand against her belly. "I went to

Jeremy—that—that was his name . . ." She paused and Stephen nodded. "I told him about the will . . . and also that I was going to have his baby. He . . . wanted me to end the pregnancy. It was Mrs. Broom, our old house-keeper, who gave me the fare money to run away, and I ended up in Coudersport."

"Remind me someday that I owe Mrs. Broom a great thank-you."

He watched her blush at his words and reached across the small table to take her hand in his. It was becoming increasingly clear to him that spending a lot of time alone with her in the remote cabin was not going to be a *gut* idea. Even now he wanted to make love to her. He closed his eyes briefly on the thought, then got to his feet with abrupt movements.

"Ella—I—uh—I need to go over to the spring for a bit. It's just a stone's throw away. Don't worry about cleaning up."

He knew she was watching him with confusion, but he could not explain to her that he needed the cold water against his skin—anything to distract him from his unpredictable and tantalizing thoughts . . .

Ella tidied the small eating area quickly, then did her best to fasten her dress with the proper pinning. She was innately curious as to what Stephen was doing at the spring and decided with youthful reasoning that there would be no harm in following him.

She walked out of the cabin and carefully latched the door behind her, then set off in the direction of the spring, which Stephen had indicated the previous evening. She stopped near some leafy bushes, surprised at what she saw. Stephen was kneeling on the ground near the mossy rocks and the freshwater spring that poured from the mountaintop. His eyes were closed and he seemed to be praying.

For Ella, it felt like she was intruding on a very intimate moment, more intimate than any scene of him bathing at the spring. *What does he pray about?* she wondered. And immediately on the heels of this thought came the fear that perhaps she was a burden on him, despite all that he said.

She tiptoed back to the cabin and set about making the bed and tidying up the quilts that Stephen had used during the night. Before she was through, Stephen returned with an air of quiet about him. The knees of his black pants were muddy, but he smiled at her and made some murmured excuse. Then he grabbed a second pair off a peg in the wall. "I'll change out back and then we'll *geh* fishing, if you'd like?"

"I've only fished from a jetty in the sea."

He laughed. "Well, I can't offer you so stimulating a view, but the pond down the mountain is always pretty nice."

She nodded, still wondering what might truly be going on behind the sea of his eyes . . .

Chapter Twenty

He walked beside her in the bright morning light, carrying two fishing poles in one hand, while with his other, he carefully supported her arm. It was shaping up to be a beautiful day and he felt a sense of renewal as the birds sang and butterfly moths danced before them. He wondered at Ella's quietness until she suddenly broke the warm silence.

"I have to confess—I saw you at the spring," she said contritely.

He smiled down at her. "Saw me praying?"

She nodded and he thought for a moment. "Well then, I'll have to confess that I had originally gone to the spring to cool off from—wanting you. But when I got to the spring, I realized that trying to care for you and the baby was something I needed *Gott*'s help with—I was praying to have strength when you need me. And I suppose I believe that you can store up prayers in Heaven, like savings in a safety deposit box." He shrugged, feeling insecure. "I probably sound strange."

"I think you sound wonderful, Stephen. More candid

and wonderful perhaps than even my father was about his prayer life."

"*Danki*, Ella. That is something I'll treasure."

She stopped still and stretched to kiss his cheek before they went on. "I guess you're right about praying," she commented as he adjusted the fishing poles in his hand. "If we'd pray a bit every day, I guess our lives would be that much richer."

"*Jah*, and perhaps our children's lives and our grand-children's." He realized that he was probably being too exuberant and clammed up, lamely trying to change the topic of discussion to relatively safe tales of fishing.

Ella carried on a mundane conversation with Stephen all the while that it seemed her heart was beating like a hummingbird's wings. She wondered, deep inside, if he'd been talking about their very own children and grandchildren—it was a heady thought. But perhaps he was simply talking in general. She resolutely decided not to ask for clarification—and besides, his thinking certainly didn't need to be consumed with her . . . That was vanity! So, she concentrated on her footing instead and was glad when they reached a pretty pool of water.

She waited while Stephen found a comfortable and safe rock for her to sit on, baited her hook, and helped her cast her line in. She had a large rainbow trout out of the water before his line even hit the pond.

"Sorry," she apologized sweetly. "Papa always said I was a good fisherman."

"I should say so!" He smiled. "All right, Lady, you're on your own from here on out. I'll just sit over here and keep an eye out for bears. They sometimes come down to the stream to fish too!"

She laughed and it felt enormously good. For the first time in a long while, she didn't feel edgy or afraid. She felt safe and cared for—even with Jeremy she had never felt like this. She threw Stephen a saucy look as she pulled in another nice fish and basked in the Amish man's approval.

Sunday morning dawned clear and bright and Stephen helped Ella pin her hair into a proper bun, but not before kissing the back of her neck in a sultry manner that left him faintly gasping and not especially in a hurry to *geh* to church meeting. But Stephen knew that Joel would expect them there on time, so he led Ella out of the cabin and onto the trail.

They walked in companionable silence until Stephen took a branching path that led off the trail and they emerged at the edge of a hayfield. "This is Franz Stolfus's farm. The service will be held in his large barn. We move around twice a month so that everybody in the community who can has a chance to host. And then there's usually a big picnic dinner afterward."

"Oh, good!" Ella exclaimed, and they both laughed together.

Stephen was glad when Joel and Martha came to greet them. He knew from the way she clung to his hand that Ella was just as nervous as he felt inside. *Ach*, he didn't mind what people thought, but the last time he'd stood in front of this community, he'd been accused of murder . . . Still, Joel was bishop now, and he and Martha were kindness itself. When Stephen would have reluctantly left Ella sitting with the other single women, Martha spoke up clearly.

"*Nee*, Stephen. Ella is our guest for today; she can sit by me for company."

Stephen gave Martha a grateful look, then smiled encouragingly at Ella before he took his place standing behind the benches with the other single men. *It's a funny thing though,* he thought to himself. *I don't feel that single anymore. I feel—married to Ella* . . . He would have considered this revelatory thought more, but just then the service started with the two traditional hymns. Soon, Stephen was lost in the familiar, soothing church time, but his eyes strayed often to where he could see Ella sitting, and he wondered if the backless benches were too uncomfortable with her pregnancy.

Then it was time for Joel to bring the message, and Stephen shifted his weight on his legs, wondering what his friend would talk about. Then Joel began.

"The Bible says that '*Derr Herr* was a Man of sorrows and well acquainted with grief.' I often think to myself of the things that grieved Him, made Him sorrowful, and do you know what? Those things are quite often exactly what trouble us on occasion. Now I will say with certainty that we have not been hurt to the extent that He has, but we all know what it is to be lonely, alone, restless, lost, broken, and worn. And chances are, if you have not experienced these feelings and times in life, you someday will—not as a cruelty or punishment but simply because sorrow and grief are often part of this life—and, if you look very, very closely with the eyes of your heart, these things might even come to be gifts, initially disguised . . ."

Stephen smiled at the blessing *Derr Herr* had provided to Joel. His friend was able to address difficult subjects and lay them before the community in a positive light. Suddenly Stephen lost his worries about appealing to his neighbors. All would be well . . .

* * *

Viola felt Esther bristle beside her at the bishop's words. *No doubt Esther has felt these things herself, but she will not yield her heart or her mind to what* Gott *might give . . . And how much more do I hold back—from my own* sohn . . . Viola felt tears fill her eyes and quickly swiped them away, but her eyes filled again and again, until she was forced to borrow Esther's handkerchief . . .

Ella sat listening intently to Joel's earnest and inspired words. She'd gone to church services in Cape May with her father, of course, but rarely had she paid as much attention to the sermon as she did now—even when she'd listened to Pastor Rook in Coudersport.

She considered all of the things that had happened—many of her own choosing—over the past few months and knew for a certainty that God had brought her here, to Ice Mountain, to shelter her in the palm of His Hand. She looked down at her Amish dress and then over at Martha's kind profile and knew that there was no mistaking her thoughts—*God brought me here . . . us here . . .*

She placed a gentle hand over her belly and then looked up in time to see Stephen striding to the front of the barn near Joel. She was wondering what this part of the service was about when Martha reached over to grasp her hand in an affirming touch.

"You all know my friend, Stephen Lambert," Joel said. "And I understand that there's been talk since Stephen has returned to the mountain about what his role in the community may be and who the *maedel* is that he brought along with him. I think it best if Stephen explains himself."

Ella watched Stephen's face and felt her heart begin to

speed up. She wanted to help him in some way, especially because he stood up there alone to defend her. But then Martha gently squeezed her hand once more and Ella calmed, remembering her thoughts of peace and comfort of only a few moments ago.

She sat up straighter and began to pray in her mind, softly and with confidence, that Stephen would know exactly what to say . . . Stephen glanced at Joel and nodded briefly before turning to face the Amish community of Ice Mountain.

He wanted to throw up, but he wanted to get this over at the same time. And he didn't want to cause Ella any discomfort. He began softly, then cleared his throat. Finally, his voice rang out steady and true.

"You all know me, but perhaps you do not know me well. Some words may come to your minds as I stand here—I know they come to me: wild, bad, drifter, murderer . . . shunned. Well"—he smiled—"I'd like to ask you all to put aside those thoughts for a moment as I request your help and offer what I can to the community to help you. I've been working as a firefighter in Coudersport and I've learned a lot about structural fires. Consequently, I have learned what makes a good structure—so I can both fight fires and build. I can also help you learn what to do or not do to prevent fires in—our—community. I also would like to ask for sanctuary for a time for the *Englisch maedel* I've brought back with me." He sought Ella's dark-eyed gaze, then went on slowly. "Ella Nichols is pregnant, as many of you may know. She was deserted by one who claimed to love her but did not, and I guess we can all understand that a bit—perhaps many of you have felt unloved for at least a moment in your lives . . .

Anyway, she needs help—protection—from her *aenti* and *onkel*, who live far from Ice Mountain by the sea. They want to be sure Ella never shows up again because she is the rightful owner of the home she grew up in, not them. I would ask you for this favor but have you know that there's risk involved to your own safety—Ella and I have already stopped one man from harming her . . . or I should say that *Derr Herr* stopped him. So I offer this plea humbly and would ask you to remember also what it is to be Amish and to remember that we were once hunted in the Old Country ourselves . . . *Danki*."

He waited, never taking his gaze from Ella. The silence seemed interminable. Then Sol Kauffman, the big store owner, boomed out a response.

"Sure and why shouldn't we give safety to the *maedel* and her *boppli*? And firefighting is something I'd like to know more about from young Stephen here."

"*Jah*," Herr Mast, an elderly member of the community, agreed. "It is not right to turn away a mother in need."

Stephen listened and soon a myriad of voices were raised in affirmation and he had the absurd desire to cry.

Then Joel broke in. "I think you have your answer, Stephen. Thank you for shedding light upon your and Ella's situation. As bishop, though, I would ask one thing . . . Perhaps it would be more fitting if Ella were to remain in the home and care of our new local schoolteacher, Miss Christy King, and her *mamm*. This, I think, would give you a chance to help us build a fire brigade, Stephen. In addition, you can then freely move about the community and be on the lookout for anything suspicious."

Stephen stared daggers into Joel's blue eyes, but Joel merely shrugged and returned a sunny smile. Finally though, as well-wishers of the community surged forward to greet him and Ella, who had joined him, he saw the ironic humor in his *gut* friend's move. *Joel is forcing me to choose whether I want to court Ella—formally . . . and I could wring his neck . . .* He felt Ella's tentative pull on his shirtsleeve and glanced down to reassure her. "It'll be all right, Ella," he whispered to her quickly. "You'll see."

It was only after the crowd had thinned that he got Joel alone for a moment while Ella spoke to the young school-teacher and her *mamm*.

"Some friend you are . . ." Stephen began.

"I am the bishop as well as your friend. Besides, don't you think that Ella deserves a proper courtship? I have no doubt you've been—uh—poaching upon her lips on more than one occasion."

Stephen gave him a sour smile. "You've seen it for yourself."

"There we have it, then." Joel slapped him on the back, and Stephen slapped the bishop's back in return—hard.

Chapter Twenty-One

Ella discovered, much to her pleasure, that Christy King was a cheerful, charming young teacher and that her mother had a spirit to match. The two women enveloped Ella in a cocoon of comfort and grace that left her feeling like cherished china.

The King women lived in a small cabin not too far from Sol Kauffman's store, and it was only later on the same night as the church service that Ella had a chance to begin to truly miss Stephen. She lay tucked up in a thick featherbed and stared out of the small bedroom window at the dark sky of the evening. She thought back to when Christy King had gently led her out of the barn and away from Stephen; she'd felt as if she were losing a lifeline. But he'd flashed her a beautiful smile—a you'll-be-all-right smile—and she'd clung to that memory throughout the afternoon and evening.

She'd tried to help set the table for dinner, but Christy's mother, Mercy, had waved her away from the simple, pale blue plates that were stacked at the ready. "*Nee*, my *maedel*, *sei se gut*, sit down. You've enough work to do in carrying the *boppli*." Mercy had smiled with a tender expression, as if remembering when she'd been pregnant.

Ella had wondered where Mercy's husband was but didn't ask the older woman, and his absence wasn't mentioned.

She'd sat down to a delicious meal of roast beef, creamy mashed potatoes, and sugar snap peas, fresh from the kitchen garden, while dessert was blueberry cobbler. Ella'd had hardly any room in her tummy after the meal and had been glad to sit at a small side table with Christy while she prepared some work for the Amish students for the following day.

Christy had given her a good-natured smile when she'd stared with interest at the array of papers, showing many different levels of work.

"How many grades do you teach?"

"It's all one class with students of all different ages, and this is our last week of school. I teach first through eighth, and then the students spend a year learning a trade or staying at home helping to learn to run a farm or household."

Ella had thought back to her father's desire for her to study art, but she'd wondered if such a thing would even be thought of among the Amish. When Christy had passed her a pencil and some paper to lay out some cursive letters, Ella had automatically begun to sketch as her attention wandered. Without thinking, she had seen in her mind's eye the piratical curve of a fine mouth and dark hair and deep-set sea blue eyes, as well as an aquiline nose and quirk of black brows. She had started abruptly when Christy leaned over to peer at her efforts.

"It could be no other than Stephen Lambert, though we Amish tend not to see ourselves drawn or photographed."

Ella had stared down at her sketch. "I—I'm sorry. I

meant no offense." She had moved to tear it in half when Christy stopped her with a quick hand.

"There's no offense given, and how could you know, in any case? Besides, perhaps you'd like to keep the sketch as a memory for when time passes by."

Ella had nodded, quickly folding the drawing and placing it in her apron pocket. But Christy's light words came back to her now as she lay in bed. She moved from beneath the beautiful, rose-colored quilt that covered her and crossed the room to where she'd hung her apron on a peg earlier. The paper rustled in her hand, and she knelt down in the light of the moonbeam that crossed the hardwood floor to study the face that had become so dear to her. Her friend, but perhaps so much more . . . Yet the sketch and Christy's reaction to it raised many questions . . . *There is much that I don't know about Stephen and his people, and perhaps it's wrong to presume upon his friendship . . . I am not Amish, despite my dressing as if I am, and Stephen deserves to have someone in his life who knows who he is at heart and what his values are . . .* She ruthlessly pushed thoughts of his tenderness from her mind and reminded herself that he'd brought her to Ice Mountain for her safety . . . not for any romantic reasons, despite his kisses . . . She sighed, then glanced up, alarmed, when a gentle tapping sounded outside the window above her head. She felt the grip of fear clutch her heart . . .

Mitch Wagner lay on his cot in the Coudersport jail. The night air drifted in with the pleasant smell of honeysuckle through the bars on the window of his cell and he drew a deep breath of contentment. It mattered little to him that he faced trial for arson—he knew now that although he must pay the consequences for his act, the Lord had already forgiven him.

He sat up when he heard the police chief's chair slide back across the cement floor with the accompanying sound of a jangle of keys. The police chief was probably back from supper. Mitch had grown used to a visitor or two during the evening time—usually either Lester Pike or Pastor Rook—each bringing words from the Bible to cheer and encourage him as he faced an uncertain future. But tonight he heard the unmistakable sound of a scuffle and the grunts of two men engaged in fighting. Mitch stood near the bars of his cell and was trying to look down the brief corridor when there came a solid thump, as if someone had hit the floor hard.

Mitch blinked as a few seconds later a match was struck in the hall and the smell of cigarette smoke drifted near. Mitch saw a tall, blond-haired man in a fine suit approach his cell.

"Mitch Wagner?" the other fellow asked as casually as if they'd met on the street.

"Yeah. Who are you?"

"It doesn't really matter except for the minor fact that I'm here to end your incompetence."

"Huh?"

The younger man laughed and jangled the ring of keys he held. "Come now, let's get you out, shall we?"

Mitch watched in strange fascination as the man undid the old-fashioned lock on the cell door, then dropped the keys to the floor with a jangling crash.

Mitch considered the new peace he'd found in life and shook his head slowly. "I ain't going."

"Of course you are." The stranger laughed low as he withdrew a small revolver from his pocket. "Now, move."

Mitch's right arm slashed out and his fist connected with the man's cheek just as the gun went off. Mitch grasped his side and fell back in time to see the man grind his cigarette into the floor, straighten his hair, and walk off down the hall, leaving him for dead.

Mitch knew, through a haze of pain, that whatever it cost him, he had to somehow find Ella Nichols and her baby before the city slicker did. And he staggered with determination out of his open cell.

Stephen tapped softly on the glass window of the Kings' spare bedroom and was pleased when he saw the fall of Ella's red hair, but then he noticed her expression of fright in the bright moonlight.

"It's me," he called, pressing nearer the glass. He didn't want to make a scene and wake the King women, but he badly wanted to see Ella, to talk to her and touch her and to remind himself that even after so short a separation as an afternoon, she was real . . . *I'm probably narrish*, he thought as he watched her white fingers carefully slide open the window.

"Stephen? You scared me half to death. Are you allowed to be here?" Her whispered words made him smile.

"*Jah* . . . why?"

He watched her bite her bottom lip and longed to soothe the spot with his tongue.

"Well, I thought Joel said . . ."

"Joel wants me to court you—if you'll have me, that is." He waited, held in tight anxiety, not realizing how much her answer would mean to him. But he saw puzzlement rather than acceptance on her sweet brow.

"What does 'court' mean to the Amish?" she asked tentatively.

"Courting is—a time to get to know each other better," he began. "A time to see if maybe—we want to spend more of our life together."

Her face cleared and she gave him a brilliant smile. "Oh, well, that would be wonderful. In fact, I was just thinking that I'd like to know more about you and about your people's ways."

He nodded, feeling both relieved and joyous at the same time. Then he heard the rustle of paper and leaned into the window, resting his forearms on the sill. "What do you have there?"

She laughed, clearly flustered. "This? Oh, it's nothing . . . I mean . . ."

She looked all of about fifteen with her hair flowing down her white *nacht*gown and the mysterious paper tucked suddenly behind her back.

"Should I climb through the window and find out for myself?" he teased.

"No . . . Anyway, I'm sure that's not proper courting behavior."

"*Ach*, you might be surprised."

"I didn't court . . . before," she confessed, pressing a hand against her belly.

He wanted to gather her in his arms and make her forget that any other man had ever existed, but instead, he found himself praying for the right words to say to her. After a moment, he cleared his throat. "Ella . . . I don't want some phantom man you did or did not court to be between us . . . as we court. In truth, every day that I have with you feels fresh and new and so full of promise that part of me has to be glad for all that . . . Jeremy wasn't, because that gives me the opportunity to be those things."

She tilted her head to one side, as if considering his words, and then stepped closer to the windowsill. "Did you ever court before, Stephen?"

Against his will, he thought of Rose Raber, whom he'd once considered courting. Then an image of diminutive, dark-haired Laura Keller, the young widow in Coudersport, rose up before him. But even his zeal at being with a woman for the first time didn't match the consuming feelings he had for Ella. Before he could respond, Ella ran a fingertip along his bare forearm, where his green shirtsleeve was rolled up.

"Because even if you did court someone, Stephen, I am no fool . . . I benefit from whoever taught you to kiss."

Amazed at her candor, he felt himself flush and was glad for the cover of shadow and moonlight that hid his face. "*Danki*, Ella . . ." *But I'd be glad of a lifetime to practice with you* . . . He pushed aside the thought of what the future might bring and concentrated on the moment at hand. "Bend closer, sweet Ella, so that I can display my—talent at kissing once more."

She complied with a shy tilt of her head and he reached to run his fingers through her long, soft hair until he found her shoulders. He kissed her slowly at first, deliberately holding back until he heard the sweet whimper of want come from the back of her throat. Then he pulled her closer and kissed her with hard, deft strokes. He ignited a fire in himself that he knew needed to be slowed to a smolder, because kissing through a window was inconvenient, if not downright uncomfortable. He pulled away and sucked in some hard, deep breaths; then he smiled at her as she stood with her eyelashes half resting on her creamy cheeks and her mouth looking delectably red and swollen, even in the moonlight.

"Maybe I should tell you more about courting in the Amish culture," he whispered with a pained laugh.

"All right," she sighed. "Tell me about Amish courting."

"Well," he began, ducking his head to lay his chin on his arms, "we could start with bundling." He swallowed as she gently touched his hair and tried to concentrate on her words.

"What's bundling?"

He cleared his throat. "It's really quite an old tradition. Sometimes it's called 'bed courtship,' but it isn't as intimate as it sounds . . ." He was watching her face as she studied him with interest.

"So we lie in a bed together?" she asked, eyeing him in the moonlight.

He pushed aside the physical longing her innocent question conjured up and smiled at her vaguely. "Something like that . . ."

"I thought that the Amish were supposed to be . . . well . . . conservative."

"We can be." *We . . . we* . . . the word didn't sit quite right with him, and he looked down for a moment.

"Stephen—what's wrong?" He felt her ease her fingers around the back of his neck, and he shivered, then swallowed hard. He glanced up to meet her dark eyes.

"I—I don't know if I'm Amish—I mean, really a part of this community here. I've always felt—like I was some wild thing . . . existing on the fringes of what everyone else considered to be normal." He blew out a breath of frustration. "I mean, I know that Joel and Martha accept me, but my *mamm* and . . ."

Ella knelt so that their faces were level. "Stephen— you came back here to protect me . . . It's not worth it if it's causing you this much distress."

He half smiled and reached to run his thumb down her soft cheek. "I think *Gott* wants me to have this out here— on Ice Mountain—this battle within myself, once and for all. And your protection is my privilege, sweetheart."

He leaned forward by inches so that his forehead touched hers. "You should not be kneeling so, with the baby . . ."

But Ella silenced his mouth with a bold intention, drinking from his lips until he felt like a sweet blackberry wine, and he forgot his protests about her position for a long while . . .

Chapter Twenty-Two

"Well, whoever he was, he wasn't a great shot—fortunately for you. Even though it was fired at close range, the bullet only grazed you." Mitch drew a deep breath as Nick stitched calmly and closed the bloodied gunshot wound with a few stitches.

"Thank ya, Doc."

Mitch felt the weight of the other man's gaze and resisted his normal habit of looking away. He knew now that his True Father was in Heaven and that he was His son, so he had no cause to feel worthless inside.

The doctor finally spoke. "If what you tell me is true, the chief was only knocked out cold. The police will be searching for you, but for some strange reason, I believe you when you say that someone is after Ella—and consequently that Steve is in trouble too. I know where they are and I'll take you there, but if you do anything to hurt my friend, I'll take your stitches out . . . with my teeth."

"I understand," Mitch said solemnly.

And Mitch remained solemn as Nick loaded him in the back of his car and covered him with a dark blanket. They were nearly out of town, as far as Mitch could tell, when the car was stopped and a flashlight played over the inside of the automobile.

"Dead man."

Mitch heard the doctor's laconic explanation and prayed that he wouldn't be found out. "Cover me, Dear God," he whispered against the wool of the blanket.

His prayer was answered as the doctor was given leave to drive on. After a few minutes, Mitch sat up halfway. "Can you tell me where we're going to, Doc?"

"A place called Ice Mountain, and I suggest you take a quick nap, because the car will only get us so far."

"All right." Mitch lay back down and closed his eyes, praying even as he rested . . .

Ella finally left the window once Stephen had gone and crawled back into bed. She shivered with chilled delight beneath the quilt and felt her mouth and cheeks with her fingers, loving the sting that Stephen's faint beard had left on her skin. As she drifted off to sleep, she found herself asking God, with a stumbling petition, if He would bless Stephen and keep him safe. It felt awkward but right and she slipped into a deep, dreamless sleep.

Stephen sought the path to Dan's cabin with familiar ease in the deep dark of the woods and was glad to strip off his shirt and pants and fall into bed. But the pillow held Ella's scent from the *nacht* before and he tossed restlessly before slipping into a vivid dream . . .

The young widow, Laura, stood before him, beckoning him near. He found her mouth, his hands skimming the curve of her waist before he lifted her. He closed his eyes

*and saw a blur of color and then it was over, and he felt
strangely alone . . .*

He sat up in bed, his body soaked with sweat. He realized by slow degrees that his mind had supplied Laura in his dreams because it was safer than letting himself be with Ella . . . *Ella, whom I've dreamed of before, but now she seems closer to my heart . . . What did Nick say? That I have a problem getting truly close to a woman, probably because my* mamm *made me feel like a wretch . . . I can do the lovemaking—the work of the body and mind—but my heart has been closed somehow, until Ella . . .*

He looked up from the tangled sheets when a heavy knock sounded at the cabin door.

"Steve? It's Nick . . . and, uh . . . Mitch."

Stephen grabbed his pants and hastily made himself decent, even while he questioned frantically *was en der weldt* his friend was doing on Ice Mountain with the arsonist. He flung open the door and stared out at the two men in the moonlight.

"What's the matter? Is it Ella? I should have stayed with her—I knew it—"

"Steve, calm down. Ella should be fine." Nick made to shoulder past him, but Stephen caught his arm.

"What do you mean should be fine? Is she—is it the baby?"

"Steve, look, let us in. Don't you have a light in this place?"

"What? Yeah . . . let me get it . . ." Stephen turned up the lantern, then faced his friend. "Now, what is going on?"

Ella was pleased when Christy asked the next morning if she'd like to go to school and help her for a bit. Frau King sent them off with cloth-covered lunch pails and molasses cookies bigger than Ella's hand. They rounded the general store, and Ella chewed her treat with delight and still had more to go when they climbed the neat steps of the school*haus*.

The students came in shyly as they noticed Ella sitting by the teacher's desk. She smiled with gentleness at the group, sensing their suppressed excitement. Miss Christy rose to speak to the assembled children and introduced Ella with warmth.

"And, Ella, you'll be able to understand most of what we say, because the Bishop wants us to practice our *Englisch* for the end of school program this coming Friday. Pretty much all of Ice Mountain assembles for a morning of student performances and good things to eat."

Ella saw a dark-haired boy with big blue eyes raise his hand. He spoke in clear tones as Christy acknowledged him.

"Teacher, will we get to ate—I mean, eat, too?"

"After your recitations, *jah*." Christy smiled. "Yes! Now let's show Miss Ella the class quilt we've been working on." She pointed to a half-assembled paper square quilt on the large blackboard. "You see, I asked each student to paint a square that shows what the word 'home' means to them. We'd be honored if you'd like to add one yourself, Ella."

Ella nodded and forced a smile. She was suddenly overcome with the urge to cry, though she couldn't quite explain the reason. *Perhaps it's because the first thing I think of when I think of home is no longer the sea but rather the blue-green of Stephen's eyes . . .*

Then Christy handed her a crisp white square of paper

and indicated the paint table and some paint smocks. "We don't usually paint, but this is a very special quilt."

A quick knock on the back door of the school*haus* made everyone look up in expectation as Christy went to answer it.

She was back in moments, and Ella held tightly to the fabric of a smock as Christy smiled at her in a distracted fashion. "Miss Ella . . . it's Bishop Umble. He asks to see you for a moment outside."

Ella nodded and put the smock down, then slipped along the side aisle. She had the vague feeling, from the silence in the room, that she was being called to the principal's office or worse as she tried not to worry that something might be wrong with Stephen. She got to the door and allowed Joel to take her arm and help her down the steps.

"What is it?" she whispered. Then she blinked in the glare of the morning sunlight and saw Stephen standing a few feet away with his arms crossed. Mercy King, Christy's *mamm*, was there—as well as the doctor from the Coudersport Hospital and the strange man who'd been sent to do away with her. Ella didn't ask any more questions but broke free from Joel and ran to Stephen with a dry sob. He caught her close and held her tightly, despite the onlookers.

"Stephen, oh Stephen . . . I've missed you so much since last night." She realized then as he released her gently how her words must have sounded to the bishop and the others. She turned and lifted the hem of her apron to dab at her eyes. "Courting, I mean. We were courting."

Joel smiled. "It's all right, Ella. Don't worry. Look, I thought we all might take a little walk together and talk."

She stared up into the sea of Stephen's eyes and watched him nod. "*Kumme*, sweetheart. All will be well. You'll see." She felt his long fingers twine around her hand and she knew she had to be content to wait to see what was going to happen.

Stephen clasped Ella's delicate hand and wished there was some way to spare her the information that was to come. He himself could scarcely believe the message of the would-be assassin. Furthermore, he had no idea why Joel wanted them to walk to the creek, but he knew enough about his gifted friend to understand that there must be a point to it all.

They all walked together until they came to a path that led to the meandering creek. Joel invited each of them to take a seat on the large stones that marked the boundaries of the water.

Stephen sat down and unceremoniously pulled Ella into his lap, looping his arms around her. He watched her freckled profile turn to where Joel stood and then he resigned himself to listen as well.

Joel balanced on a rock and spoke out with an obvious plan in mind. "What a strange lot we appear to be—gathered here together. But we all have things in common . . ."

Great, Stephen thought. *He's going to preach—but . . . maybe I need the lesson.*

"We have in common our basic humanity, our need for love, and our need for *Gott*—whether we're aware of it or not. And each of you have come to Ice Mountain in one way or another to protect Ella, here, and her baby."

Stephen couldn't resist tightening his arms around Ella, and he felt a tenderness in his heart when she leaned back against him, relaxing somewhat.

"But," Joel continued, "I want you to know—especially you, Frau King—that we don't expect you to put your own lives in danger, no matter your first feelings on the subject."

Mercy King's kind, older eyes met Stephen's and she nodded. "Christy and I will be fine, Bishop Umble. It is our pleasure for Ella to remain with us. We do not fear, for *Gott* watches over us."

"We appreciate that, Frau King," Stephen said formally. "But the bishop knows that I have more than a vested interest in Miss Ella, and I think she'd be safer with me."

Nick snorted and Stephen shot him a scowl. "What?"

"You're not thinking clearly. He wouldn't go to a schoolteacher's house first."

Stephen was about to respond to his friend when Ella spoke up. "'He'? Who are you talking about?" she asked, and Stephen hated to see the pulse throbbing in her pale throat as she got worked up. He reached out, beneath her *kapp*, to rub soothingly at the base of her neck.

"Don't fret so, Ella," he whispered.

"He's talkin' about the fella that shot me last night," Mitch Wagner said softly, and Stephen wished him gone when Ella's heart began galloping.

"It's all right, Stephen," Joel said clearly. "Why don't we let Mitch tell what he knows?"

Stephen nodded with a jerk of his head and waited until Mitch seemed to find his words.

"Ya see, miss." He looked at Ella. "Your friend, Lester Pike . . . well, he and Pastor Rook have been comin' ta the jail regular-like. Anyways, they've shown me who the Lord is and I'm a changed man. I wanted to try and talk ta that fella last night, but he shot me right quick and wouldn't tell me his name. I couldn't let him hurt you or the baby—I jest couldn't . . ."

"What did the stranger look like, Mitch?" Joel asked softly, and Stephen gave his old friend a keen glance.

*Joel knows already—it's his second sight or whatever.
He knows by sight the man who wants to take Ella's life . . .*
Stephen almost said something, but Joel gave him a brief,
almost imperceptible shake of his head.

Mitch went on. "He was a city slicker type, real thin,
and had on a suit and tie, and blond hair that it seemed
like he fussed over . . ."

Stephen felt the words as clearly as he heard them
when Ella cried out. "It's Jeremy . . . I know it is!"

Chapter Twenty-Three

Ella struggled to her feet from Stephen's arms. She felt a cold, nervous chill despite the summer sunshine and wrapped her arms about herself as she paced the ground. In as few words as possible, she explained who Jeremy was, too upset to even mind what these people might think of her. She wanted to hide against Stephen's lean chest but refused to go near enough to be held.

Then she turned resolutely and looked up into Stephen's eyes as he rose to stand near the rock. "I need to leave— now. I cannot lay my troubles at your doorstep—any of you. It's my fault and my poor judgment that have brought me to this and I—"

"Ella?" Mercy King had risen to her feet and took a few steps closer to her. "Ella, perhaps you've never paused to wonder why there is no Mr. King in our *haus* or where Christy's *fater* might be?"

Ella focused on the smaller woman's form and shook her head slightly.

"Well," Mercy said gently but firmly, "I was a nineteen-year-old girl. A *gut* solid Amish girl, as I thought—one who was determined to marry a *gut* solid Amish man—until that summer when a roving *Englisch* man came to Ice Mountain. *Ach*, how I thought I was in love with him. And—as *Gott* would have it, following what you might call my poor judgment, I found myself *mitt kindt*—pregnant." Mercy drew an audible breath, and Ella had a strange foreboding in her stomach as the other woman continued her story.

"I was sure that I would follow the *fater* of my *boppli* around the *weldt* or welcome him here into our Amish world if he would have it. But . . . to my surprise and horror . . . the man was a monster in disguise. Wanted for the murder of two other young girls, he'd stumbled upon Ice Mountain as a hiding place, but my *bruder* heard news of him down Williamsport way and brought back a sketch of the man—it was him—the *fater* of my *boppli*."

Ella felt her eyes fill with tears as she stood riveted to the pine needle floor of the forest. "How did you get away from him? What did you do?"

"My *bruder* brought the *Englisch* police here but there was a shootout and my—the man—he was shot and taken from here to Rockview prison in Bellefonte. He screamed at me as they left that he'd be back one day to kill me and the baby . . . For a long while, I believed it and lived in fear, thinking that every day would be my last. But then, *Gott* spoke to my heart and told me that fear was no way to live. So I choose to live another way—one of faith and trust—and I've brought Christy up with both the truth about her earthly *fater* and the Trueness of *Gott*. Her true *Fater*."

Ella couldn't speak for a moment and was surprised when Mitch Wagner rose to his feet and put an awkward hand out to touch Mercy's sleeve. "She's done right, living knowin' God that way. And—and I've come to know God meself as Father . . . both a Baby and a Father." He nodded at Ella and Mercy, then dropped back to his stone seat after a moment.

Ella weighed the words of the man who had tried to take her life and felt a deep sense of connection with the Amish woman who'd shared such a dark yet victorious story of faith. She was about to speak when Stephen's friend Nick threw a stone into the creek with an abrupt movement.

"This is all fine and good, and I'm genuinely sorry for your past, ma'am"—the doctor nodded at Mercy—"and your triumphant living today . . . But I'm here to make sure that my friend Steve is going to be all right in this whole mess."

Ella saw a small smile appear on Joel Umble's face as he glanced at the doctor. "Perhaps it's not as much of a mess as you might think."

Stephen shifted restlessly on the steps of Dan's old cabin as he struggled to wait until it was truly dark. *Joel or no Joel . . . bishop or* nee . . . *I'm going courting with Ella tonight* . . . Not that Joel had forbidden any such thing, but he had insisted that Ella stay with the King women. Stephen had gritted his teeth and agreed, knowing that Joel wanted him to trust *Gott* with Ella's safety . . . but the truth was that he wasn't very *gut* at trusting. He was used to being the rescuer . . .

He looked over his shoulder as the cabin door opened behind him and Nick stepped outside. Stephen moved over on the steps to make room for the doctor.

"Your bishop is an interesting fellow," Nick said without preamble.

"And a good friend," Stephen agreed softly.

"He wants me to stay on Ice Mountain until tomorrow afternoon instead of going to Coudersport in the morning . . . seemed very specific about it."

"Well—" Stephen shrugged absently. "Joel usually has a good reason for asking what he does."

"Like letting Ella stay at the schoolteacher's house?"

Stephen exhaled slowly. "Yeah . . . probably that too. But . . ." He rose to his feet. "That isn't going to stop me from checking on her. So . . . don't wait up."

Nick laughed shortly. "Do you think I'm going to sleep on the floor in there with the first guy who wanted to kill Ella?"

"Use the bed," Stephen offered, his mind already leading him into the intimate shadows of the *nacht* and his time with Ella . . .

Ella waited, fully dressed and *kapp*ed, for the signal of a pebble against the cabin's bedroom window. She felt jittery with nervous excitement at Stephen's promised coming and she had very nearly turned up the kerosene lantern further when the noise against the windowpane came with a discreet sound.

She hurried to the window, having a last-second doubt that perhaps it could be Jeremy out there, when Stephen's dear face appeared outside the glass within the halo from the lantern.

Ella gave a soft cry and put the lantern down, then carefully lifted the window open. Stephen smiled at her, then slung a long leg over the low window sash and climbed inside. He closed the window and turned back to gather her into his arms.

"Oh, Stephen. For a moment, I feared that it might be—"

He swooped down and covered her lips with his in a brief, hard kiss. "Don't say it. *Sei se gut*, Ella, let's not worry tonight. Tomorrow, you know that Joel and Nick and I will find that scoundrel before he does any more damage."

"Well, I'm afraid for you," she whispered, rubbing her fingers down his shirtfront.

"Then let me distract you," he said with a husky laugh. "*Kumme* . . . I see in the rafters that Mercy King has a board we might use for bundling—if you'll allow it."

Ella felt a delicious shiver run down her back, and she felt a tightening in her belly that caused the babe to kick. "Yes," she replied simply, in contrast to the myriad of warmly entangled emotions that pulsed through her.

"*Gut. Danki*, Ella." He kissed her tenderly, then moved to stretch up and slide the fairly long, thin board from the rafters.

He placed it on its side, using the top quilt to hold it in place. She felt the hot weight of his sea green gaze as he turned and held out a hand to her. "Let me help you lie down."

She took his fingers and then followed him to the bed. He helped her lie down on her back, and she tucked her arm awkwardly along the quilted board. She watched Stephen come round the other side of the bed, then settle himself against the opposite side of the board. He leaned up on one elbow and smiled down at her.

"You know, Ella, that bundling is actually puritanical in nature—meant to cool the lust of the body with conversation instead. In fact, I know a bundling poem, if you'd like to hear it."

She raised herself up on her side of the bed and smiled at him, glad he was obviously trying to make her feel comfortable. "Please let me hear."

Stephen gave her a faintly wicked grin, then glanced upward as he recalled the words.

> *"'Some maidens say, if through the nation,*
> *Bundling should quite go out of fashion,*
> *Courtship would lose its sweets; and they*
> *Could have no fun till wedding day.*
> *It shan't be so, they rage and storm,*
> *And country girls in clusters swarm,*
> *And fly and buzz, like angry bees,*
> *And vow they'll bundle when they please.*
> *'Some mothers too, will plead their cause,*
> *And give their daughters great applause,*
> *And tell them, 'tis no sin nor shame,*
> *For we, your mothers, did the same.'"*

Ella laughed softly with him, then reached her arm over the board and let her fingers trace the contours of his face with feather-light strokes, skimming his thick eyelashes and high, flushed cheekbones, then moving lower to touch his lips—firm yet tender. He opened his mouth and drew her index fingertip inside.

She was shocked at the sultry, wet touch of his tongue and then he began to suck and she felt her nipples harden. She closed her eyes and drew a deep breath when he edged his teeth over her tender skin, alternating the burning movements of his mouth and tongue until she felt a strange ache deep inside. She squirmed against the board, wanting something, but she wasn't sure what. And then he stopped and she couldn't swallow the soft cry that came, heady and high, from the back of her throat.

* * *

Stephen tried to control the pulsing rush of blood that thrummed through him. He knew he was playing a dangerous game with his senses, but he had a reckless desire to continue—*It'll keep her mind away from Jeremy* . . . He tried to ignore the fact that her obvious reaction to him simply sucking her fingertip promised a responsiveness that overwhelmed anything he'd ever experienced before. And he wanted to share with her . . .

"*Ach*, Ella . . . you're so beautiful."

He saw the gleam of appreciation enter her eyes and her voice took on a teasing note. "Beautiful yet pregnant?"

He laughed low. "Beautiful and pregnant. Now talk to me about something so that I might be distracted from your beauty and your body."

"All riiight, I tried buttered noodles today for supper."

"Mmmm . . . buttered noodles." He had the irreverent thought that he'd like to slather her in cream and taste . . .

"Stephen, are you listening?"

"Of course. What did you say?"

She giggled and he was struck by how intimate and cheerful a sound it was. *Have I ever laughed with a woman so easily? I could spend a lifetime doing so with Ella . . . a lifetime . . .*

His train of thought shook him, and he wondered at himself. *Do I love her? Is this what love feels like?*

"What's troubling your mind, Stephen?"

He saw the concern on her face and shook his head. "Nothing. Just thinking about the next way to kiss you . . ." *Right . . . you coward . . .*

Ella looked at him in surprise. "Are there other ways to kiss?"

Her innocent question spurred his desire, but he

nodded warily. *Bundling . . . talking . . . that's what we're supposed to be doing . . . Not teaching her things like the ways to kiss . . .*

But she looked so genuinely interested that he thought one more kiss couldn't hurt.

"I've heard the girls at the Social Club in town talk about French kissing, but if that's when you stick your tongue in my mouth till I gag—I'm not interested in that one." Her tone was flat and he choked back a laugh. But then he realized that some other idiot had kissed her in such a fashion, leaving her uninterested if not plain disgusted.

"Ella," he asked earnestly, "did Jeremy . . . uh . . . kiss you like that?"

"Yes." She nodded so vigorously that several stray tendrils of red hair escaped her *kapp*.

He reached to tenderly place them behind her right ear, then thought about how best to proceed. He'd spied a wooden bowl of fresh blueberries on the table by her bed when he'd entered, and now he got to his knees in the center of the bed, leaning against the bulk of the quilted bundling board.

"Ella, can you reach me those blueberries?"

She looked confused but nodded her head. "Of course." She rolled over a bit and brought back the berry bowl. He took it from her, then offered her a hand.

"Now, will you kneel like I'm doing?"

She complied easily and he stared down into her steady, dark eyes as he lifted a plump berry from the bowl he'd placed beside him on the bed.

"*Gott* made our mouths, agreed?"

She nodded, clearly wondering where he was going with the topic.

"And He made our lips—to kiss." He took the berry

and rubbed it lightly across her lips, trying hard not to notice the fact that her breathing had become shallower and faster.

He leaned closer to press his lips against the side of her neck. "And he made our tongues, sweet Ella, to touch, and twine, and lick . . ." He punctuated each word with a damp kiss and felt her pulse throb against his mouth. "So . . ." He knelt back upright. "Somebody kissed you like a fool and I would remedy the situation, if you'll allow?"

She nodded with limpid-eyed eagerness and he swallowed hard against a wash of desire. He took the blueberry and held it up before her gaze, then gently and purposefully crushed the fruit until drops of juice appeared on his thumb and forefinger. "Open your mouth a bit," he encouraged, then rubbed the juice across his own lips and bent close to her once more, steadying her with his hands on her arms.

"Now," he whispered. "Taste me with your tongue . . . and tell me a secret."

He felt the muscles of his back tense when she leaned in with a dainty tongue tip to lick at the juice droplets, and he suppressed a groan. "Kiss and tell. I'll have your secret now."

"I used to steal red tulips from the beach cottage next door."

He casually reached for another berry. "*Ach*, flower thievery . . . Did you remember to shake off the dirt from the stems?"

She smiled. "No . . . not always."

"Wicked child. So, now you, sweetheart." He passed the berry into her warm fingertips and waited while she seemed to consider the fruit with a calculating eye. He watched her squeeze the berry and his heart sped up. She trailed the juice across her pink lips and he waited.

"Taste me with your tongue and tell me a secret, Stephen Lambert."

He leaned forward and let his tongue play between her lips for a long moment. When he pulled away, he felt like he'd run a long mile in a winter's field.

"And your secret?" Ella asked softly.

He stared down at her as trivial confessions vied with truth in his mind. *My secret . . . I love you . . . I love you . . .*

Chapter Twenty-Four

A pink sky was the early morning backdrop for the mountain, warning of a storm to come later that day. Mitch Wagner was both surprised and happy that the Amish bishop had asked him for an early-morning walk.

"So yer like the preacher hereabout?" he asked Joel as they set out on one of the myriad trails that Mitch couldn't keep straight. He was too used to the concrete and bustle of a town, even though he found Ice Mountain to be a strangely wonderful place of peace.

"Preacher?" Joel Umble replied. "You could say that. Why do you ask?"

Mitch gestured with an awkward hand. "Well . . . all you Amish seem to be peace-loving and calm inside—must have a pretty good preacher to have those things going on."

"*Danki*, Mitch. But the Amish are just like any other people—we get jealous, angry, sick to death of each other . . . you take my meaning. In any case, I wanted to walk with you today to ask what your feelings are about helping to search for this Jeremy Collier . . . After all, he's shot you once."

Mitch laughed. "Without much aim, and I guess the Lord was watching out for me. But I don't mind helping at all. I know that I've got charges to face and prison also for setting that fire and even thinking of hurting the red-haired missus and her baby. I'd like to see this Jeremy fella in a cell next to mine. Maybe I could try and talk some sense into him."

They walked on and Joel satisfied Mitch's curiosity about different birds he heard calling and the names of plants he'd never seen before. The trail broke after about half an hour and the bishop pointed across a wide field to some small wooden cabins on a hill.

"The Ice Mountain Amish own those little cabins. We usually rent them out this time of year, but no one's come asking yet."

Mitch shrugged in wonder as he gazed at the beautiful space. "Must be like heaven livin' up here."

Joel clapped him on the back as they turned to the trail. "Heaven? Well, you might just be right, at that!"

Ella was helping Mercy wash berries that morning and she had to try to hide the flush she knew burned her cheeks when she thought of her time bundling with Stephen the night before.

"There's a bad storm coming," Mercy murmured, breaking into Ella's heated thoughts. "You can feel it in the air."

"Oh, yes." Ella smiled. "It reminds me of the sea. You can always tell when a storm's coming, and I used to love to listen to the wind and the rain."

"*Ach*, not me! I'd rather scrub the floors than hear a storm. But since you aren't afraid and the clouds seem far away for now, perhaps you wouldn't mind taking a quilt pattern over to Martha Umble? Stephen's due to be here soon and he can walk with you, just to be on the safe side."

"Oh, I'll be glad to go see Martha. I liked her from the moment I met her."

Mercy smiled. "She is a beautiful young woman, and I don't mind risking vanity in saying so." She went over to the neat desk against the living room wall and brought a carefully folded pattern back to Ella. "It's a baby's quilt . . . maybe you two might start one together, seeing how Martha's due at the end of summer as well."

"I'd love to!" Ella smiled with enthusiasm. "One thing I can do very well is sew, and I'd love to try my hand at an Amish pattern."

"Well, here's a cookie—sugar and cinnamon today. Why not wait out on the porch for Stephen?"

Ella accepted the large round sweet with pleasure and nodded happily. She went outdoors, pleased that Mercy was not so worried about Jeremy that she would try to keep Ella indoors, especially when the wind was beginning to whip about.

She waited for a bit, then decided that she knew the way to Joel and Martha's, or at least had a sense of the direction. She decided to set out before it began to rain, thinking she would probably bump into Stephen on the way.

The first flash of lightning cracked the gray sky with eerie yellow light, and Ella hurried her steps and was glad when she caught sight of the large Umble cabin. She followed the wooden slatted walkway and climbed the steps, giving an easy knock just as the first raindrops began to pelt the ground.

Martha opened the door with a cheerful smile, and Ella shivered with anticipation of the storm as she was urged inside.

"I've brought the quilt pattern Mercy had for you," she explained.

Martha laughed. "*Gut*! I've got so many squares that we can share and make our quilts together while we talk. I hope you will stay for a while. I know that Joel went out to meet Stephen and the *Englischers* a bit ago. So, we can have some fun!"

Ella was only too happy to agree.

Stephen met Joel and Nick along one of the paths. "Where's Mitch?" he asked.

"I asked him to keep guard at the trailhead," Joel said. "Are you stopping to say *gut* morning to Ella, or do I even have to ask?" Joel teased over the rising storm.

"Don't ask," Nick snickered, and Stephen punched him in the arm good-naturedly.

"I only want to check on her."

"Right." Nick rolled his eyes. "And I want to meet May Miller before I leave and see what herbal healing secrets she knows—and I'd like to get there before we're soaked."

Stephen nodded as the rain began to stream down in sheets. "You two go on to May's. I'll only be a minute at the Kings' cabin." He practically had to shout over what was now a deluge, and soon all three men were running along the path.

Stephen gained the front porch of the King cabin and watched the other two men pound merrily along in the now-muddy way. Stephen turned and knocked on the door, wiping at the rain that dripped from his hair with a quick hand.

Mercy answered the door and looked up at him in obvious surprise. "Stephen, where's Ella?"

"What? I thought she was here."

"She was about half an hour ago. She came out onto the porch to wait for you. I asked her to take a quilt pattern to Martha."

Stephen tried to slow his heartbeat and pushed down a feeling of alarm. "Don't worry, Mercy. She's probably at Martha's right now. I'll backtrack and check."

"Well, *sei se gut*, let me know."

"I will." He stepped off the porch and waited until Mercy closed the door before he broke into a run in the direction of the Umble cabin.

Ella had the uneasy feeling that something was wrong with her new friend when Martha kept shifting positions on the old, comfortable couch where they both sat sewing.

"Martha, are you all right?"

"Hmm? Why, *jah* . . . I just can't seem to get comfortable. Maybe if I stand up . . ." Martha got to her feet, and suddenly something splattered to the floor. Ella leaned forward and stared in horror at the small puddle of blood that had come from between Martha's legs.

"*Ach*, dear *Gott*, the baby," Martha whispered.

Ella stood up and forced herself to speak calmly. "All right, Martha. It's all right. I want you to lie down on the couch here. Come." Ella helped her lie down and automatically put a pillow between Martha's legs to try to slow the bleeding.

"I'm going to go get help, Martha . . . Maybe Nick is still on the mountain—he's a doctor."

But Martha shook her head with a sudden pained gasp. "*Nee* . . . don't leave me, Ella . . . *sei se gut* . . . I know I'm miscarrying."

"You don't know anything for sure right now." Ella gulped back a sob as more blood appeared. But she knelt down to take Martha's hands in hers.

Ella looked up in alarm a moment later as the front door banged open and Stephen stepped inside, dripping wet. She watched him take in the situation at a brief glance.

"I'm going for Joel, and May Miller and Nick."

Ella was glad for the calmness of his voice as he turned and ran back out into the rain, and then she began to pray.

The storm had passed, leaving a welter of young rose petals on the Umbles' porch steps. Stephen stood, numbly leaning against the banister rail, while Joel sat, staring out at the dripping trees. Ella was inside. Martha had asked for her while May and Nick finished up, and Stephen struggled to find something to say to his best friend.

"We will call him John," Joel said with a definitive nod of his head.

"That's a *gut* name."

"*Jah* . . . *gut* name."

"Listen, Joel, I'm so sorry. You know I love you and Martha both, and if there was anything that I could do—" Stephen stopped. Words seemed senseless in this grief. He decided he could only sit with his friend and listen.

After a few minutes, the screen door was eased open

and May Miller came outside carrying a carefully wrapped, very small bundle. Stephen saw the tightness in her usually calm features, and he swallowed hard as she bent to give Joel the baby's body.

She slipped back inside and Stephen felt his eyes fill with tears as he watched his friend tenderly feel beneath the soft covering.

"His face is small but he has a *gut* nose, I think. Would you like to see?"

Stephen nodded and stepped forward, then dropped to his knee beside Joel's chair. Joel showed him the dear little face, then bent his head as thick sobs of grief wracked his body. Stephen reached out and encircled his friend with his arms, and they cried together.

"When will they have the funeral?" Ella asked Stephen listlessly as they made their way back to the King cabin later that afternoon.

She was exhausted, mentally and physically, and was grateful for Stephen's arm around her waist.

"Probably the day after tomorrow," he said after a moment.

She nodded, then whispered solemnly, "I don't understand, Stephen."

"Neither do I . . . but Joel seems at peace, sitting there with the little fellow. He and Martha will grieve together, and Ice Mountain will mourn with them."

"Martha was so calm. I was terrified."

"Of course you were," he said soothingly. "I felt the same when I ran for Joel to *kumme*."

"Martha was so kind to me—after. She said that *Gott* would bless me and my baby, and she seemed as though she herself had been blessed even though it was such a loss."

"Joel and Martha are special people, I guess. They don't always see things from an earthly perspective but rather from the long-range view of heaven."

She glanced up at him. "Thank you, Stephen—for listening to me and giving me perspective. I think I got the best end of the deal when I jumped out of that fire and into your arms."

He shook his head. "*Nee*, that was my privilege and my pleasure. And, Ella, I want you to know that—"

A sudden, strange click sounded on the air and she looked up to realize too late that they had approached Mercy's cabin and that Jeremy sat smiling on the front porch in a hickory rocking chair, an ominous revolver pointed directly at them.

Stephen stopped, the way he did on a trail when a big yellow rattlesnake lay sunning itself across the path. His first instinct was to tell Ella to run, but he realized that might put her in more danger, so he stepped in front of her instead.

The thin blond-haired man on the porch snickered. "My, my, Ella Nichols, if you haven't found yourself a defender . . . But I have no need for an Aimish superman. You—" He waved the gun briefly. "Step away from the girl—oh, and her brat."

Stephen knew that he had to remain calm. If nothing else, he wondered vaguely where Mercy King was and if she was still alive. Jeremy Collier seemed reckless, and he looked half-deranged from what was probably lack of sleep.

"Jeremy," Ella cried. "There is no will . . . no letter from my father. They were burned to ashes in a fire at my boardinghouse just weeks ago. Uncle Douglas and his wife own the Sea Castle without dispute. You can go back and tell them so!"

Collier laughed. "Do you really think I'm that stupid? If I show up without your pretty red head on a plate, I lose out on the stuff of life—money, my dear. Now shut up—your talking always did bore me."

"Look, why don't we settle this like men?" Stephen asked low, hoping to stall for time or at least get Jeremy away from one of the most-trafficked paths on the mountain, one that was very near the school*haus*.

"Like men?" Jeremy got up from the rocker and walked down the steps. "Well, why not?"

He pulled the trigger without any further warning, and Stephen felt a blinding surge of pain in his right upper arm. He wavered on his feet and heard Ella's scream from far away. But then, he was able to refocus in time to see Mitch Wagner come into view behind Collier with a shotgun in his hands.

"Drop the gun, buddy." Mitch's voice was clear and steady, and Jeremy froze for a moment, but then he reached out and snatched Ella to him. He put the gun to her temple, and Stephen waved Mitch off.

"Now," Jeremy said with a devilish laugh. "Everybody just back off. This little piece of fluff is going with me, and the first man to interfere signs her death certificate."

He had started to drag Ella off the path when Stephen saw her suddenly turn and ball up a small fist. She hit Collier's wrist, and the revolver went flying. Mitch moved forward and snatched it up, but Jeremy suddenly pushed Ella to her knees, then rushed at Mitch Wagner. The air was rent by his strange, garbled cry. Mitch fired the revolver and Collier stopped cold, then fell to his back on the sun-dappled ground.

For a long moment, everyone was still as a bubble of spittle and blood appeared at the corner of Collier's mouth. Stephen wanted to know whether Ella needed any last words with the man, but he'd passed away too quickly for such an opportunity.

Instead, he cuddled her close as Joel and some of the elders came to hear the tale. Stephen had even forgotten his gunshot wound until Nick pulled at the frayed edges of his shirt. "You need some attention, Steve, even though it looks like the bullet passed clean through."

Stephen nodded, prepared to *geh* to May Miller's, but then Joel called for everyone's attention.

"Friends—today has been a difficult day for many of us, but I want to suggest something. Of course, I'll leave it up to you all, but *Gott* tells my heart that this is right. Today, we'll bury an attempted murderer—one whom Ella tells me had no family that she knows of—well, I'd like to make the suggestion that the man we bury is not Jeremy Collier but rather Mitch Wagner."

Stephen heard murmurs of confusion and Joel held up a weary hand. "Mitch Wagner started a new life in the jail at Coudersport. I'd like to let him continue it. Ice Mountain offers many things, but over in the little cabins on the side hill, we offer the chance for redemption for a man who's determined to change his life with *Gott*'s help."

Stephen lifted his voice in support of Joel's suggestion; he had great respect for his friend. Soon, others joined in with their points of view and in the end, Mitch Wagner was given free rein to stay in a little cabin of his choosing, where he would take a new name and make a new life, and Jeremy Collier was buried with quiet dignity near the Amish cemetery. Stephen noted that even Nick kept his mouth shut during the whole process and no doubt would go back to Coudersport with some new views of the Mountain Amish.

Chapter Twenty-Five

It was nearly a month since little John Umble had been buried by a reverent community, and Ella had found an ever-deepening friendship with Martha. This day in early July, they sat on the wide, welcoming porch of the Umble home and drank limeade while talking and watching Joel and Stephen in the field with Joel's sheep.

"Have you heard back from your uncle regarding the will and his, um . . . plot to kill you over it?" Martha asked.

Ella had to smile. The whole situation seemed so strange and remote now. "I heard from his lawyer and I waived any and all rights to the Sea Glass Castle—not that I could have proven right of ownership anyway."

She felt Martha's thoughtful gaze and turned to look at her friend. There were gentle lines that only conquered pain can bring about Martha's beautiful eyes and a soft seriousness to her mouth, but otherwise the joy of God had made the death of John pass by on angelic wings, and Ella once more felt a deep gratitude for the opportunity of knowing the Umbles.

"You sound comfortable with the idea of giving up

your home by the sea?" Martha's tone was questioning, and Ella turned so that she might better see Stephen in the field.

"I suppose there are many seas in life," Ella murmured, thinking of Stephen's eyes and then blinking in surprise at her words. "I mean, uh—"

Martha laughed softly. "I think often lately of the Bible verse 'The Lord giveth and the Lord taketh away—blessed be the name of the Lord.' It comforts me and I think it might comfort you too."

"Oh, yes." Ella turned and smiled. "I remember my father quoting that line, but I haven't thought of it in a long time. It is comforting. In truth, I suppose that I always thought the sea would be my home, but here . . . Well, Ice Mountain has a beauty and a people all its own, and the Lord has provided that for me through Stephen."

"Well, I've learned since John's death that life is too short not to ask questions, important questions of those we care about. So I'll ask you, Ella, why do you still wear Amish dress? It isn't that anyone minds or that I take offense in any way . . . I'm just curious."

Ella felt herself flush, despite the kindness of Martha's tone, but then Martha reached a hand out to her and Ella squeezed the slender fingers with gratitude.

"I wear the clothing because I guess it gives me the feeling of belonging. Maybe in my heart—I'm afraid that I don't."

"And you want to?" Martha asked softly.

Ella nodded, blinking back sudden tears. "Yes . . . and these past weeks, Stephen and I have been courting, but he's—well—he's pulled back some, physically I mean, and I suppose that is one of the major ways that we communicated before. Now . . . everything seems emotionally quiet and still. I don't know . . . Perhaps he's sorry that he's saddled with me and I should go."

"*Ach*, no, Ella. From what I know of Stephen, I'd say he's thinking everything through very carefully. You know, one of the best ways to belong to Ice Mountain is to marry into the community. Maybe he's thinking of that."

"I don't know . . ."

"Would you wish it if he were?"

"I'm not even sure whether or not he wishes to belong for himself. You know he has barely spoken to his mother or aunt for a long while."

Martha nodded. "Joel has said this. But—I guess—in the end, it is *Gott* Who will arrange what happens, and for the best. You can be sure of this, Ella."

Ella bit her lip and Martha squeezed her hand. "What is it?"

"Martha, ever since John's death—even the day you—he—you've been so calm in your spirit, so certain that God has the best plan for you and Joel. How can you believe that when, to the world, everything looks so difficult?"

Martha smiled gently. "I'm no saint in my thinking, believe me . . . but I know that *Gott* loves us, that He's for us, and that I will see little John one day again. That makes it all enough. Joel is coming in from the field now . . . why not *geh* out and walk with Stephen? There are some beautiful trails in the woods near the pasture."

Ella caught her friend close in a tight hug and nodded. "I will do as you say. Thank you, Martha."

Stephen playfully rubbed the side of Joel's favorite sheep, Lost Lenore, while Sophy, the Umbles' frisky white dog, pranced in and around the sheep's spindle legs. Stephen looked up as Ella approached and held her gently with his eyes. Her body was beginning to show the definitive shape of her advancing pregnancy, and she looked incredibly beautiful to him. Still, he knew his behavior of late during their evening courting was probably puzzling to her—it was confusing enough for him!

Ella drew up on the opposite side of Lenore, and a slight breeze pressed the fabric of her yellow dress against her abdomen. Stephen wanted very much to lead her into the cool darkness of the copse of trees that bordered the field. He longed to run his hands over the pronounced fullness of her breasts and find the secret curves that her pregnancy had advanced and kiss her throat and . . .

"Stephen?"

He blinked and looked rather dazedly down into her dark eyes.

"*Jah?*"

"I was just talking with Martha—she asked me something. But that's not what matters now. I want to ask you—oh, a lot of things . . ." He watched her delightful nose wrinkle in confusion and knew that he was going to have to face up to some things he wasn't even sure of himself.

"Ella . . . I know I've been different the *nachts* I've come calling, but I've wanted to try not to overwhelm you with—well, too much of the physical. I wanted to let you have room to think and for us to talk more and get to know each other."

"That's all good—though I miss some of your—uh—physical ideas. Like blueberry kissing . . ." Her tone was wistful and he felt a sudden pounding of his blood at his pulse points. He was about to reach for her when Sophy's shrill barking sounded from the woods and the sheep moved restlessly away.

"Ella." He said her name with quiet firmness. "I want you to turn and walk quickly back to the porch with Martha. Don't run and don't look back. No matter what you hear. Now, *geh*."

He saw the confusion on her face but something of the eerie urgency he felt must have translated itself to her, and she turned and began to walk as he'd told her to do.

Sophy was silent now and Stephen sensed that something had happened to the little dog. Was it even worth taking a quick look round the woods? But he decided to try. Joel and Martha needed no more sadness in their lives.

He crossed the remainder of the field and entered the woods, his nose already detecting a particularly musty odor that gave him the clue that he was no longer alone in the woods. He moved forward slowly over the spongy ground and saw Sophy lying, bloody and whimpering, directly ahead of him on the path. Her plumy tail lifted once in brave salute and he whispered softly to her. He risked a step further and saw the bear, a huge bruiser of an animal that held a dead sheep in its paws as though it were a toy.

Stephen moved to scoop up Sophy and the bear growled low, clearly feeling threatened with its stolen food. Stephen held the little dog close and began to back away but the frustrated bear was faster. Stephen felt the slash of a fast paw graze his head and face, and then everything went dark . . .

Ella watched the closed bedroom door of the Umbles' spare room and prayed over and over again in the silence. *Please God, let him live, let him live, let him live . . .* She felt Martha's hand reach out and cover hers, and she knew that the other woman was praying too. Ella bowed her head and willed herself not to cry but the memory of Joel carrying Stephen from the woods was almost more than she could stand.

Then the bedroom door opened and Joel appeared, looking so pale that the bones of his face stood out in stark relief. "Ella," he said softly. "Will you come? He's asking for you."

Ella squeezed Martha's hand, then released it as she got to her feet. Her heart was pounding so hard in her ears that she couldn't hear her own footsteps as she crossed the wood floor to what had hastily become the sick room.

"He was fortunate," May Miller said shortly as Ella moved close to the bed.

Raw, even stiches stood out in what would eventually become a jagged scar along one side of Stephen's face and head. The metallic smell of blood hung heavy in the room and Ella couldn't help but notice that his chest also bore several oozing, stitched wounds.

"Most of the slashes weren't too deep, though he'll have scars for sure." May rinsed her hands in a basin. "He's feverish already. The bear's claws carry all sorts of bacteria, but we've cleaned the wounds thoroughly; now he just requires close nursing. I could get someone I know to do it," the healer offered.

"No," Ella said stoutly. "I'll nurse him. Joel can help me lift him to change bandages, but I want to be the one who takes care of him."

"*Gut.*" May gave her a brisk nod. "But do not overdo. You must take care because of your pregnancy."

"I won't do too much," Ella promised, suddenly realizing that she badly wanted everything to go well with the baby because it would make Stephen happy. It was almost as if the child were his. She marveled for a moment at the transformative thought, then longed to be alone with Stephen so that she might soothe him.

He cried out for her, already beginning to move restlessly among the quilts on the bed, and Ella went to the bedside and began to gently dab at his forehead with the compress that May had abandoned. "Stephen," Ella said clearly. "It's all right. I'm here."

He opened his blue-green eyes briefly and she moved her face near his. "Are you all right?" he choked out, and she gave him a brilliant smile.

"I'm fine, Stephen. The baby's fine. And even Sophy will live. You just sleep and think about getting better now."

She watched a faint smile appear on his lips; then he obeyed her and closed his eyes.

Word of the bear attack spread over Ice Mountain and Joel himself, as bishop, called for a special time of prayer for Stephen to be held in the Umbles' barn. Esther, Stephen's *aenti*, said that it was foolishness to assemble to pray when each might pray at their own home, but Viola Lambert dressed soberly, covered her head in a dark bonnet because of the pouring rain, and slipped out of the *haus* to begin the walk to the Umbles'.

As her sensible shoes sloshed through the mud puddles, she was surprised to be joined by an *Englisch* man walking down from the high timber.

"Evenin', ma'am," he said politely, over the noise of the rain.

Viola nodded, realizing that this must be the *Englischer* who'd once threatened Ella's life but who had now made a major change in his way of living.

"I used to be known as Mitch; it's Mike now—the

bishop asked me down to pray for Stephen Lambert. You goin' there too?"

"*Jah* . . . I—I'm his *mamm*."

"Oh—I didn't know. I'm sorry about his run-in with the bear. It's scary to think that those creatures are roaming these woods. You must have been scared to death."

Viola weighed the kindly spoken words in her mind. "Scared"? "Terrified" was more like it. She knew in her heart that she could no longer continue to hold Stephen at arm's length when his very life might hang in the balance. She knew then that, while most everyone was at the prayer time in the barn, she would need to *geh* to the Umbles' *haus* to see her *sohn* in person.

"*Danki*," she murmured to the man, then hurried ahead of him in the rain toward her *sohn*'s bedside. That was where she belonged.

Chapter Twenty-Six

The smell of summer rain drifted in through the screen window in the Umbles' guest room. Stephen watched Ella through half-open, bruised eyelids and wished for the hundredth time that his pain might ease some so that he could kiss her. But May Miller's pain-relieving herbal tea kept him somewhere between lassitude and the gnawing feeling that he'd been hit by a truck. He was grateful when Ella approached the bed with the small spoon and cup—evidence that it was time for another dose.

He swallowed the noxious medicine, sip by sip, from the spoon, glad that Ella's closeness afforded him the fresh scent of her as well as the vision of her rounded breasts, pressing through the light lavender of an Amish dress. He gazed up into her dark eyes and wondered if his scar would make any difference to her. As far as he knew, she had been intrigued by his appearance, but surely his face would cease to be at all attractive after the bear swipe.

"Don't, Stephen," Ella whispered gently. She put the spoon and cup down, then bent to place her hands on either side of his head. She smiled into his face, and he forced himself to open his eyes wider. "Don't worry about how you think you might look. You will always be beautiful, and I'll bet the girls will only like you more for the character your scar gives you."

He had no idea where they came from, but hot tears filled his eyes at her kind words—almost impersonal in nature. "*Nee* other *maedels*," he managed to whisper hoarsely. "Only . . . you."

He saw her blush, and it satisfied him in place of what she did not say. She understood his concern, but did she return his feelings? He parted his lips, intent on telling her that he loved her, when there was a hesitant knocking at the door. He wanted to yell when Ella eased from the bed but closed his eyes instead, intent on ignoring whoever it was . . .

Ella opened the bedroom door, expecting it to be Joel or Martha, and found Stephen's *mamm* instead. Viola Lambert looked up at her with shuttered eyes and a hesitant expression.

"How—how is he?"

Ella widened the door. "Please come in—please. I was about to go and get some more cool water. He's been running a bit of a fever, but the wounds look pretty healthy according to May Miller."

"*Danki.* All right. I'll come in . . ."

And Ella closed the door behind her gently, giving mother and son some rare time alone.

Viola inched toward the bed, not wanting to wake him. She found she was infinitely glad that he was asleep.

Perhaps I can say all that I want and he need never truly know . . .

She sat down on the edge of the chair Ella had drawn close to the bed and let her gaze sweep over the bandages and bruises and the flush on his face surrounding the wicked-looking scar. She clutched her hands together in her lap and sought for a place to begin.

Strangely, she recalled a time when Stephen had been little more than a year or two old and Ben had felt that their *sohn* was troubled by nightmares, unusual in one so young. Viola smiled tremulously at the memory, then wet her lips.

"Your *fater* loved you," she whispered. "So much so that once, when you were little more than a babe in arms, he feared that your sleep was troubled by *nacht*mares . . . He called for Dutch Wolf, the *auld* healer of Ice Mountain, to *kumme* and see to you. Now, Dutch was a strange man, or so folks said . . . but when Ben told him about you, Auld Dutch came and took a broom and used it to sweep the four corners of the ceiling of your room. The healer said he was sweeping away all of the *nacht*mares that hung over your cradle." Viola paused for a moment, seeing the old-fashioned twig broom laid against the ceiling in her mind's eye. She smiled faintly. "And then there was the time you were teething real bad. Your *fater* sought out Dutch Wolf once more and the *auld* man told Ben to *geh* and kill the big yellow rattler that was sitting on a triangle-shaped rock by the stream and to bring back its rattles. Sure enough, there was a rattler, and sure enough, Ben brought the rattles home and pinned them on your tiny *nacht*gown because Dutch said the rattles would scare away the pain . . . *Ach*, Stephen, how I wish I could take away all of your pain now. As well as all of the pain I've caused you over the years . . . But there is no magical spell to break the lost time we haven't had. And there is no *fater* anymore to seek comfort and a cure . . . If only you could know how very sorry I am. How wrong I've been . . ." She choked on a hoarse sob, then nearly startled when his dark head turned on the crisp pillow and he studied her silently with intense blue-green eyes.

"Stephen—I—I thought you were asleep."

"Don't . . . hide," he whispered. "I hear the sorrow in your voice, Mamm. We can . . . start again." His tan hand slid across the quilt top toward her and she took his fingers gently into hers. She laid her head down to wet his hand with her tears of gratitude and love.

Ella reentered the quiet bedroom once Stephen's *mamm* had left and found him staring absently at the window.

"Stephen? Are you all right?" She slid into the small chair beside the bed and leaned close to him.

He nodded, and she felt along his forehead for fever, then sat back with a sigh. "Joel has brought the community together to pray for you out in the barn this evening. He just told me that they would pray for me and the baby as well. I am so blessed by your people—I do not even know where to begin saying thanks."

She watched his sea eyes focus, then narrow at her words, as if he was in pain, and she caught up a cool cloth to ease against his brow. He winced away when she dabbed too near the stitches on his temple, and she dropped the cloth back into the basin.

"I'm sorry," she murmured. "Would you like a cool drink of spring water?"

"*Nee* . . . I want . . . you to know . . . They're not just my people . . . Do you think of them as yours as well?"

She looked into his eyes, bright with fever, and sought

a way to tell him how much she wished they were her people. She began slowly, hesitantly. "Until our time here, I always thought that the sea was my home, but I know now that I want this baby to be born here, on Ice Mountain. But Stephen, what do you want? There's no reason for you to stay here to hide me from my crazy family anymore, and you could go back to Coudersport to the firehouse and your work there."

She bit her lip, unsure of the mixed emotions on his face. "Do you—want to go back?" she asked finally.

He shook his head, a brief movement, but one that still left her feeling uncertain because he did not speak.

Stephen felt frustrated that somehow she had not directly answered his question but had replaced it with one of her own. Yet hers was a fair question and one that expressed consideration for him. *Do I want to stay? Until when? Does Ice Mountain feel like home?* This last thought echoed in his consciousness, and he looked up into Ella's concerned eyes.

"I once told you that Ice Mountain no longer felt like home. But being back here, spending time with you and Joel and Martha, and even now, the promise I made to my mother to start anew—it all matters. It does feel like home . . . but it would not be complete without me telling you—that I love you. I love you, Ella."

He watched her dark eyes fill with happy tears, which she dashed away with a quick hand. "Oh, Stephen, I love you too."

He wanted to catch her close in a soulful embrace, but the best he could do with his injuries was reach out an arm, and she moved to cuddle as close to him as she could.

It came to him as he held her lightly that he wanted no

hurried wedding, even if she would consent; he knew it would be all too easy to rush into marriage because of the babe. *Nee*, he wanted more time to court and for her to think about what loving each other might mean—after all, she'd thought she loved Jeremy. And how could he marry her when she wasn't Amish? It all made his head hurt, but his heart resounded with the truth that he loved her, and for now, that was more than enough.

Chapter Twenty-Seven

"You really need to get some rest, Ella," Martha said gently. "May Miller says that Stephen is out of the woods now."

Ella smothered a delicate yawn behind her hand and smiled tiredly. "I know, but I'll give him his supper first, and then I'll lie down. I promise."

Ella went along to the kitchen to scramble some eggs and heat up some nice pieces of sliced ham. She added a bowlful of strawberries, lightly sugared, and loaded everything on a tray and went back to the Umbles' guest room, where she'd spent so many hours of late. Sophy went along with her, the little white dog now spry and happy after a week's nursing from May.

Stephen was propped up in bed, the quilts tangled around his lean hips. And tonight he looked especially handsome, even piratical, with his healing scars and the bandages removed from his tan chest.

"Hello," Ella said, almost shyly. He was like some big, lounging cat, with his tawny skin and glittering eyes, and she remembered with a slight shiver of delight what it was to have his clever mouth against her skin.

"Are you cold?" he murmured. "*Kumme*, let me warm you."

"You need to eat first," she admonished weakly as she brought the tray closer to the bed, but she soon saw that he had gained some measure of strength back when he shook his head at the tray, then grabbed a handful of the skirt of her dress.

"Stephen," she squeaked, quickly sliding the tray onto the bedside table and struggling to maintain her balance as his grip tightened by inches. She sat down on the edge of the bed and he let her dress go, only to run one of his big hands up and down the skin of her forearm. She stilled, drinking in his touch, and so very thankful to God that he was alive.

"What are you thinking?" he asked softly.

An onslaught of images and memories assailed her senses suddenly, and she felt a tightening in her breasts and belly. "I suppose I'm thinking about—us," she managed to say in a high, breathy voice that made her swallow. *I sound like some teenager, wild for the latest singer or performer* . . . But Stephen was real—not some faraway fantasy man, and she was all too happy to lean in closer to him when a smile tugged at the corner of his handsome mouth.

"Kiss me," he said.

She swiped her mouth quickly across his and then felt her spine tingle when he laughed low in his throat.

"*Ach*, so meager a kiss. Do you forget how to play, or does that bear's kiss turn my face from you?"

"I hope you're teasing. I neither forget nor do I mind the token of the bear—it serves to remind me how dear you are."

"Then, kiss me . . ."

She leaned forward a bit more, then left such a kiss

upon his lips that she thought it would surely set Ice Mountain ablaze, but his sea eyes merely held hers when she'd finished. She nearly huffed, but then she saw the pulse thudding in his throat and that his eyes had shifted to dark green in intensity. "I think I remember well how to play," she whispered triumphantly, and he nodded.

"Indeed you do, Miss Ella. But I think there might be a few more things that you could add to your—talents." He gave her a wicked smile, and she couldn't control the thrill of anticipation that washed over her in honeyed waves . . .

"So, what are your plans?" Joel asked the question idly as he relaxed in the chair beside the bed.

Stephen eyed him warily, knowing Joel well enough to understand that his best friend asked no questions without a purpose. "I thought I'd recover from the bear attack first."

"Having *nacht*mares, are you?"

Stephen gave him a sour smile. "Yeah, Joel . . . ones where I can't do what I want to do with Ella . . ."

Joel laughed. "You forget that I am relatively newly married . . . there are lots of things I like doing with Martha."

Stephen sighed, thinking of the loss of little John. "Look, Joel, I'm sorry for being *narrish* . . . I don't know what my plans are—except, late at *nacht*, when I pray, I believe I'm supposed to start a fire brigade on Ice Mountain— if some of the men would be up for it."

"I'm sure that they would. The last time we had a barn burn back a few years, I think the fire was way ahead of what we knew how to deal with."

Stephen relaxed a bit, feeling that Joel's intuitive

questioning was probably over—but he should have known that he was wrong.

"So a fire brigade—which does great good but has nothing really to do with you and Ella . . . what about the two of you?"

"Joel—what do you want me to say?" he snapped. "Do I want to leave? Could Ella ever want to become Amish? Do I love her?"

"Do you want to leave?" Joel's voice was gentle.

Stephen set his jaw and thought hard. "*Nee*," he whispered. "But how can I ever ask her to stay?"

"Well, if having my approval makes it easier—I mean my approval as bishop that she may join our faith—you've got that. And I know the community would welcome her warmly, as they've done while she's been staying here."

"*Danki*, Joel. That does help."

Joel sat upright and slapped his knees. "*Gut!* And I think the question about loving her is something you've already answered inside, many times over, my friend. You need only seek a marriage to—help things along."

Stephen swallowed, then smiled ruefully at the thought. "What's it like being married?"

"A whole lot more interesting than courting."

They laughed together as good friends do and Stephen began to plan how he might propose to Ella.

Ella was lying on the Umbles' comfortable living room couch, catching up on sleep, when she began to dream.

She was trying to walk between the great glistening sea and the intense height of a powerful mountain. She strained to fit between the two places, but her belly was too big, and she felt stuck. The sea called to her, lulling, comforting, and familiar, but she was held in check by the voice of the mountain and its strength. She lifted a hand to press it against the solid rock and felt it turn to palatial ice beneath her fingertips. She smiled and the sun caught on the display of ice and cast blue-green shadows on its form. She was comforted and loved by the subtle colors and suddenly knew that she was home . . .

Chapter Twenty-Eight

Viola packed her trunk with a calm surety. It was two days since she'd spoken with Stephen, and she knew what she had to do. One of Sol Kauffman's *buwes* was coming over to help carry her things to an empty cabin near May Miller's that the bishop said she might use. She folded one of her dresses, then looked up as Esther entered the room.

"Whatever are you doing, Vi? It's nearly time for supper."

"I'm packing. I'm leaving." There, she'd said it. Straight out.

"Leaving?" Esther's voice rose, her tone incredulous. "Where do you plan on going?"

"Somewhere where my *sohn* will be welcomed—just as he is—*nee* criticism, *nee* hatred, only love."

"You're *narrish*," Esther sneered.

"*Jah*, I am . . . for ever letting you *kumme* between Stephen and me."

"Viola Lambert, talk some sense. That *buwe* is nothing but trouble, just like his *fat*—"

"Don't say it, Esther. Ben was a *gut* man. For whatever

reason—perhaps jealousy on your part—you hated him and made me unsure of parenting Stephen."

"I came when that man died and helped you every way I could and this is how you repay me?"

Viola met her sister's cold eyes. "Here's the truth, Esther—real love never needs repayment . . . Of this, *Gott* has made me sure . . ."

Stephen tested his pain level and strength as he walked along the woodland path that led to the Kauffman store. He felt pretty good, though Ella would likely snap his neck if she discovered he was gone from the Umble *haus*. He'd left her in a deep sleep, curled up on the guest room bed after some heated kisses that had relaxed her and ignited him.

He breathed in the slight breeze that blew through the mountain laurel and it felt *gut* to be alive. He realized that he couldn't remember the feeling from anytime in the past few years—unless it was when he was kissing Ella. But life for living's sake had never been something he'd rejoiced in. His days as a youth had seemed to be made up of feeling cold, inside and out, no matter the season. And he wondered at his recent promise to his mother to "start over," but even that felt right today.

He entered Sol's store and was surprised and grateful to be hailed by the men watching the checkers match in the back.

"Hey, Stephen! Hiya! Wrestled any bears lately?"

He smiled at these older men who were about his *fater*'s age, had he lived. They were exactly the right men to lead a fire brigade and encourage the younger men along.

He walked deeper into the store, then stopped to cast

his eyes over the wooden checkerboard to see who was winning. Then he looked to Sol.

"I've been talking with the bishop, and he seems to agree with me that starting a fire brigade on Ice Mountain would be a *gut* thing."

Sol nodded in ready agreement while several other men muttered their interest. The checkers game was abandoned as the men turned to listen to what he had to say, and Stephen was struck by their willingness to learn from him.

"The last fire on the mountain was Stolfus's barn, I believe," Stephen said. "I remember I was about sixteen and helped in the water relay, as did many teenagers and women, as well as the men. We lost the barn but *Gott* was merciful and the fire didn't spread to the tree line."

"*Jah.*" Sol nodded. "Some folks dug a shallow trench to turn the fire from the forest."

"That's right, and trench turning has been around since the eighteen hundreds." Stephen paused to gather his thoughts. "I guess what I want to say is that Ice Mountain has worked as a community in the past and we will in the future. I'd just like to train all of you here so that you might *geh* out among your neighbors and train others to know what to do if there is ever a fire here in a cabin home."

"You mean like have a class, so to speak?" Pike Mast asked with interest.

"*Jah*, a class. Maybe we could even use the school*haus*, since the *kinner* are out for the summer. And anyone who wants to *kumme* can, and then they can *geh* on to teach others."

"Sounds *gut*, Stephen." Sol patted his massive belly. "And I'll bring some food and drink."

Stephen and the other men laughed together in response, and Stephen felt a flash of kinship that he'd never known before. It felt *gut* inside, and he had to leave the store quickly when his eyes filled with happy tears. *What would it have been like to have a* fater, *especially now when I could use some advice about life, about Ella?*

He smiled to himself and took a path that led back to the Umbles', pleased with the late morning's events.

Ella looked up into May Miller's face, trying to read the healer's expression as the older woman examined her for the pregnancy.

"Well," May said finally with a smile, "everything seems quite right. You should deliver within the next ten days or so."

Ella stared at her; the exciting reality of finally becoming a mother was difficult to grasp. Ten days seemed both a long time away and no time at all, and suddenly she just wanted Stephen to enfold her in his strong arms.

To this end, she bid a rather hasty goodbye to May and went out into the windy air. The mountain seemed poised in expectation of autumn, and tawny hints of reds and yellows had already begun to tinge the tree leaves.

Ella felt an exuberant burst of energy and almost wanted to spin on her toes at the smell of apples and cinnamon that she discovered Viola Lambert was brewing in a large kettle outside. To Ella's surprise, Stephen stood there too, with his *mamm*, watching as she drew the long paddle through the sugary brown bubbles of apple butter.

"This looks delicious!" Ella pronounced as she nestled close to Stephen, not even thinking of what his *mamm* might feel at her open affection.

But Viola merely smiled and offered the tip of the paddle to Ella. "Would you and the *boppli* like a taste? But be careful, it's quite hot."

Ella was about to reach out a hand when Stephen swiped a finger over the tip of the paddle then offered it to her lips. She was so surprised that she took a taste without thinking, licking the sweetness from his long fingers. "Mmmm," she mumbled, unable to control the blush that she knew stained her cheeks.

But again, Viola merely smiled and nodded her head. "Young love," she said. "It is *gut*."

Ella heard Stephen laugh, low and exultant, as he caught her closer within the shelter of his arms.

"It is *gut*, Mamm," Stephen agreed. "Good indeed."

Chapter Twenty-Nine

A few days later, Stephen insisted he was well enough to begin to teach the fire brigade classes. And it was an especially sober time as news reached Ice Mountain of the worst school fire ever to take place in the United States. It was in the city of Chicago, and ninety-two children had perished in less than fifteen minutes.

Before they began that evening, Stephen asked the assembled men to pray with him for the families of the children in that faraway place. Stephen cleared his throat and pointed out softly that a child, any child, whether it was yours or another's, felt the same as you carried it in your arms, and he prayed that Ice Mountain might never know such pain.

Then he began to talk about fire hazards and the necessity of having a plan to escape the *haus* in case of fire.

Sol Kauffman spoke up. "Why, most of us have root cellars or damp pantries below our flooring. What about going down there if we can't get out the door?"

"It's an idea," Stephen agreed. "But still smoke might get to you, and maintaining *gut* air flow is the most important thing you can do. Most folks don't die of burns but of smoke asphyxiation, so getting outside into fresh air really matters."

The class went on with various strategies and drills and ended with the resolution to meet monthly to keep plans fresh and to practice new ideas in fire strategy.

Stephen was gathering up some papers from one of the school*haus* desks when Auld Pike came up to him and clapped him on the back.

"It's a *gut* thing you're doing here, young Stephen. Your *fater* would be proud, and I'll not worry about guarding against vanity to say it."

"*Danki.*" Stephen nodded, drinking in the words. "It matters a great deal to me to think that he would be happy with my life."

"Well, *buwe*, you think on that often, 'cause it's the plain truth, and that's for sure."

Stephen took the encouragement of Auld Pike with him as he went to court Ella, who was back at the schoolteacher's *haus*.

Tonight, he crawled through the window she opened to him and he gently rubbed his hands up and down the fullness of her belly.

"What did May say today when you saw her?" he asked softly as he leaned gently against her soft form.

"Oh, not much. Ten days or so, she thinks . . ."

He backed up in surprise. "Ten days, why—that's—that's nothing. Here, sit down on the bed."

She laughed and he looked down into her dark eyes with puzzlement. "What?"

"Stephen, I'm not an egg that will crack, you know."

"*Nee*, I don't know."

He felt her press her hands against his chest, testing the

strength beneath his shirt. "May says I'm perfectly fine, and I am. I feel—oh, wonderful—like running in the ocean's tide for the first time in summer."

"You miss the sea, don't you?" he asked, reaching to stroke her hair.

"No, Stephen Lambert, I don't, because I've found twin seas of my very own, in your beautiful eyes."

He bent and kissed her once and hard. "And I've found my home in you, sweet Ella, and that means everything to me."

He tasted her mouth again, slowly, teasingly, while the *nacht* breeze stirred his senses and gave flame to his hot kisses. . . .

The sound of the school bell clanging late in the evening was always a cause for alarm on Ice Mountain, and this rainy September night was no different. And it became immediately apparent what the problem was when folks gathered and smelled smoke. Flames were already licking at the top of Sol Kauffman's store, and Stephen ran with haste to rally the fire brigade and to make sure that the Kauffman family had left the building . . .

Ella had run out of the Kings' *haus* at the sound of the bell and now circled the big store building, trying to see Stephen.

Then she heard the piteous meow of a cat, and one of the Kauffman children screamed. "Fisher! We forgot Fisher and the kitten, Mamm!"

Ella looked at the back porch doorway and saw a large cat silhouetted against the smoke and flames with something in its mouth. Without thinking about it, she recognized that this was a mother cat trying to save its baby, and something drew Ella closer to the back porch steps. The entryway looked free and clear, except for some wisps of smoke.

She nimbly ran up the wooden steps and saw that the mother cat's back foot was caught in a groove between two boards. Ella gave the cat's foot an experimental pull, and she soon had the animal loose; then she turned to head back down the steps. She'd reached the last stair when the ominous sound of wood creaking, then collapsing, echoed in her ears and she felt a hard blow to the back of her head. She staggered forward, and then everything went black . . .

Stephen watched the wood structure succumb to the fire and waved the men back as the wood burned and fell. He yanked the handkerchief down from his mouth and watched briefly, knowing that the rain would prevent any fire from spreading to the surrounding trees.

He trudged around the decimated store, the shadowy dark weirdly illuminated by the flames and the lantern light of the surrounding bystanders.

He recognized the Kauffman *kinner* standing, sobbing, toward the back of the store. One of the little *maedels* broke from the group when he met her gaze and ran to him.

He bent to the ground on one knee and caught her close. "What is it, sweetheart?"

"Your Ella went back to save Fisher!"

"Fisher—what?" Stephen's heart began to pound hard in his throat.

"Our cat and her kitten—Ella went up the back steps, but now we can't see her."

Stephen got to his feet and turned to look at the collapsed archway of the back door. "*Geh* back with your *bruders*," he told the child automatically; then he ran toward the fire. "Ella! Ella!"

He had one booted foot on the ashes covering the stairs when, mercifully, a faint cry came to him. "Stephen . . ."

He turned and ran out onto the charred grass, nearly tripping over Ella where she lay in the shadows. The eerie firelight caught on the red of her hair, turning it to flame. He knelt by her, frantically running his hands over her, assessing whether she had any injury, even as he roared for help. His fingers came in contact with the tops of her legs and he felt an ominous wetness soaking her dress.

"Stephen . . . Stephen . . . the baby. Help me," she moaned.

"Ella, just hold on. All right?" He was about to carefully lift her from the ground when May Miller loomed up beside him.

"Stephen. You've got to let her stay here. The baby's coming now."

"What?" Stephen snapped his head round to stare down at the healer and found her dark eyes to be serious and focused in the half light. "How do you . . . know?" His last word felt thin and he didn't bother with any protest. May Miller knew things, just as Joel did . . . Ella was going to have her baby right then and there.

She was conscious of looking down on herself, and of Stephen lifting her so that May Miller could spread a dark wool coat beneath her on the cold, damp ground.

Suddenly many black wool coats were piled on top of her chest until she felt a cocooning warmth seep through her bones. Someone cradled her head in a soft lap—it was Martha Umble, whispering prayers and words of comfort in tender tones.

She saw a circle of lantern light form around her as women stood bearing their lights aloft while fathers and children drifted away in the soft rain. She saw the fire dwindle slowly down to hot embers and then she felt pain that rippled down her back and around her swollen abdomen. She heard Stephen; his voice excited, focused, as he encouraged her, and then she convulsed on the ground in another spasm of pain . . .

"Wonderful job, Ella," May Miller praised her, and Ella nodded, reaching for Stephen's hand. "And here's your *dochder*."

Ella stared in wonder and fascination at the bundled infant that May placed in her arms. Surrounded by the circle of illuminated lanterns, Ella looked down into the little face.

"She's beautiful, Ella," Stephen said in abject awe. "She's got your red hair and dimples."

"*Kumme.* Enough admiring for now. We don't want either one of them to catch a chill," May said briskly. "Stephen, you can carry Ella back to my cabin to stay for a day or two."

"*Jah . . .*" he muttered.

Ella felt him bend forward, and soon she and the baby were scooped up into his strong but gentle arms.

Martha Umble stood at Stephen's elbow, and Ella's

eyes filled with tears at May's tender praise of both the baby and her labor. "I'll *kumme* see you soon, Ella."

Ella nodded, and then Stephen whisked her from the ring of lantern light to stalk across the damp earth in May's footsteps.

Chapter Thirty

Anna . . . Anna . . . Anna . . . Anna . . . The simple name reverberated around in Stephen's head. *A perfect name for a perfect* boppli . . .

It was the day after the fire and Anna's amazing birth. Ella had told Stephen the *nacht* before that Anna had been her mother's name and that she wanted to name the baby after the child's grandmother. *But what about a last name?* he wondered. *I was foolish not to ask Ella to marry me before, and then the baby would have had a last name . . . my last name . . . which would be an honor . . .*

He turned the corner of the path that led to the Kauffman store. The acrid smell of smoke still hung in the air, and he saw that the store had been gutted by the fire, along with the Kauffmans' living area at the back. He'd half expected Sol to be devastated, but instead, the older man and his wife stood talking with Joel, making measuring gestures with their hands. Stephen understood. Life went on; there was a time to rebuild. For the Amish of Ice Mountain, there was no such thing as fire insurance. Indeed, in most Amish communities, there was no insurance of any kind—instead the community pulled together and shared in the need until there was restoration.

"*Ach*, Stephen," Sol Kauffman greeted him. "We want to thank you. Without your training, we might not have gotten the *kinner* all out safely. And my *frau* here told me of Ella's delivery. How is she doing now? That girl saved our cat, and that took heart. Again, we thank you."

Stephen smiled, forgetting his fear for Ella when he'd believed she was still inside the flame-filled store. "Ella's doing well, and so is the *boppli*—Anna."

"And next, we'll have a wedding, eh, *buwe*?" Sol grinned, and Stephen avoided Joel's smiling eyes.

"I'd like to think so, but first we've got to rebuild the store and your home."

"So we do at that. I'll have to order new supplies, but the bishop here thought that we might be ready to have a store raising in a week or so."

"Jah." Joel nodded. "What do you think, Stephen?"

Stephen appreciated that Joel asked his opinion, and once again he was struck by a feeling of belonging and kinship. "I say that sounds pretty *gut*, but if you'll excuse me now, I've got two *maedels* to visit—both with the color of flame in their hair."

Ella couldn't control the blush that stole across her cheeks when she bared her breast and guided Anna to the nipple to nurse as Stephen looked on.

"You two do realize that this is something that only a husband should see a wife do?" May asked the question with a laconic smile, and Ella's blush deepened when Stephen laughed outright.

"May Miller, it could be that you've taken the very words from my mouth," Stephen said, and Ella forced herself to concentrate on the amazingly tiny fingertips that Anna fisted against her skin. But it was even more amazing when May quietly left the room and Stephen knelt next to the comfortable featherbed.

He put out a finger for Anna to grasp, then stared up into Ella's eyes. "I should have asked you before, but that makes it no less meaningful now . . . I know your dear *fater* is not here for me to ask permission of before I take your hand in mine, but I can ask *Gott* to bless the question. Ella, will you marry me? Will you both marry me?"

Ella couldn't help the feeling of joy that flooded her heart. She had never really allowed herself to dwell on the idea of marrying Stephen—perhaps because it seemed too far-fetched as a possible dream. But now, looking into his bright blue eyes, she smiled tremulously. "Yes. Oh, yes, Stephen—we will indeed . . . Only—"

"What?"

She sensed his genuine alarm at her single word and decided to come quickly to the point. "Only, I don't want you to feel like you have to propose because of Anna and everything."

She was amazed to see tears fill his eyes as he found her fingers with his warm hand. "Ella, I've spent too much time avoiding the truth that I do feel accepted here, that I am Amisch, and that I want to share my life with you."

"But I'm not Amish," she said softly. "Although I would love to join your faith if I can."

He laughed in palpable relief. "Sweetheart, Joel will have that fixed as soon as we let him, and while it's a sober thing—to join the faith—it's also a cause for celebration. And I know for sure that Ice Mountain will celebrate with you . . . with us."

Ella smiled at him in relief and knew in her heart that

what he said was the truth. Finally, she felt a great peace inside.

Stephen and indeed the whole community were stirred by the common purpose of raising the store. The new building was to sit in an area slightly north of where the *auld* structure had been, and Stephen knew that Sol Kauffman and his family were more than grateful for the outpouring of support from their friends and neighbors.

Stock was pulled by wagon from Coudersport and lumber was freely supplied by those on Ice Mountain. On a Saturday, some days after Anna's birth, the men began to gather, wearing heavy tool belts, and soon the mountaintop rang with the sounds of hammering and the good-natured teasing of the men as they worked.

Stephen searched among the women arriving later with food, looking to catch a glimpse of Ella's red hair before returning to work on a particular joist construction. He saw her and was satisfied, then returned to the work at hand.

Later, after the walls had been raised and the store began to take on a recognizable shape, an older woman rang the dinner bell, and the men surged toward the makeshift tables. The tables were little more than wooden boards balanced on sawhorses, but they got the job done, the wood nearly groaning with the weight of the food that had been prepared and brought.

Stephen found Ella trying to manage holding Anna and making a plate for herself at the same time.

"Here," he said, taking her plate. "Tell me what you'd like to eat."

"Buttered noodles," she answered promptly. "And maybe some chicken salad. That's enough."

"Ella, you've got to eat to be able to nurse."

"Shhhh," she admonished him with a smile. "I've been tasting all the various dishes all morning."

"All right. Let's *geh* and sit with Mitch and my *mamm*."

"What a strange combination of people," Ella murmured, glancing out over the arranged picnic blankets. "But good, nonetheless."

"Tell me about it," Stephen said as he guided her through the cheerful families who were already seated on various blankets.

Stephen helped Ella to sit and placed her food on the white blanket beside her. Then he sat to listen and watch as Mitch and his *mamm* made much over Anna. It felt *gut* . . . and he'd barely touched his own food before the bell sounded to get back to work.

At the end of the long day, Ice Mountain had a new store and the Kauffmans had a new home. All that was left to do was to move in the stock and set up housekeeping for Frau Kauffman. Stephen was tired and sore but well pleased to have been part of the mutual aid of his community.

Chapter Thirty-One

The following Sunday, after church meeting, Joel made the announcement that Ella had been longing to hear.

"Now friends, before you *geh*, it is my privilege to announce that Stephen Lambert has asked to marry Ella Nichols, and has gained the permission of Anna Nichols as well. The three would like this to be a community celebration, and the marriage will take place at Martha and my home in two weeks."

Ella was pleased and flattered by the buzzing of good words of affirmation around the bench where she sat. And she suddenly realized how short a time two weeks was to prepare for a wedding. She had no idea what she was even to wear . . .

"Blue," Martha said decisively later. "Amish brides traditionally wear blue. A warm sky blue would do nicely with your white skin and red hair. We'll have to get started on making your dress tomorrow."

"What else do we do?" Ella felt out of her depth. "I mean, what about the food?"

Martha waved a dismissive hand. "Everyone will bring something and the men will cook the meat."

"The men, really?"

"*Ach, jah!* Not all of them, of course, but some. And I've got plenty of celery we can cream."

"Celery?" Ella blinked in surprise.

"For good luck—though Joel doesn't believe in luck, really."

"I guess I don't either," Ella shared softly. "Because it had to be God Who arranged all of this."

Martha squeezed her hand. "Of course, it was, and He will plan the rest of our days as well."

"So, anything you want to know about marriage?" Joel asked with a faint smile.

"I'm not giving in to that trap, Joel Umble." Stephen smiled. "I have no doubt you've got plenty of sage advice."

The two friends were walking to the new Kauffman store. Sol was getting shipments of fresh stock in on a daily basis and it was interesting to see what would be coming through the door next.

Once inside, they found the store to be ordered chaos as Sol hollered and waved and directed, even while still managing to make a sale.

"*Ach*, the *gut* bishop and Stephen!" the older man yelled. "What would you be needing today?"

"Boot blacking," Stephen called back. "For the wedding."

They watched as Sol dove into a passing crate and came up victorious with a can of boot polish. "Anything else, *buwes*?"

"That's all for today," Joel said. "Except maybe some black licorice—it's Martha's favorite, you know."

They were soon back outside after many good-natured orders from Sol, directing the placement of the newly delivered goods.

"How did you know that?" Stephen asked suddenly. "What?"

"That black licorice is Martha's favorite. I'm terrified, Joel—I have no idea what Ella's favorite candy is, or anything else for that matter."

Joel laughed and clapped him on the shoulder. "Don't fret, Stephen. You will know soon enough . . . soon enough!"

Ella carried baby Anna carefully, wrapping her own cloak about the infant. She was going to Martha's for a dress fitting and was more than surprised when Martha opened the door to her and there was a sudden burst of many women's voices, raised in laughter.

"Welcome to your wedding frolic!" Martha cried, leading Ella and the baby inside.

"What? I—" Ella broke off, feeling dazed by the excitement that hung in the air.

"Normally, a bride would have a quilting to celebrate her upcoming wedding," Martha explained. "But I thought this would be more fun and more timely. Everyone's brought you a gift, so please *kumme* in and sit down!"

By the end of the afternoon, Ella was the new proud owner of a pair of candlesticks, handmade doilies for special company, carved wooden spoons, hand-tooled teethers for Anna, and a myriad of other gifts. But probably her favorite present came from Viola's hand.

Stephen's *mamm* leaned close to whisper in Ella's ear. "This is from Esther. She had a cold coming on but wanted to send you something just the same. I think she's changing, softening."

Ella opened the gift with some trepidation, half expecting scorpions or the like to jump out, but, instead she found hand-crocheted oven mitts and a small note wishing her well. It was an exciting end to an overall marvelous afternoon.

The day of the wedding finally arrived. Both Stephen and Ella and also Anna were staying with the Umbles before they would make the move up to Dan's *auld* cabin in a few days.

Stephen found himself so nervous, he couldn't properly iron his shirt and Joel had to do it for him since Ella insisted, in a very *Englisch* fashion, that they not see each other until the ceremony.

Stephen was glad for the wait, because it made the moment when he turned to look at her descending the Umbles' staircase, with Martha as her attendant, all the more magical. Stephen thought back to the moments he'd so easily trusted himself to catch Ella from the burning boardinghouse and he realized now that it was *Gott* who'd helped him on that ladder, and he was deeply thankful.

Even Joel's spiritual wedding exhortation did not speak to him as much as the thought that he himself would need to trust himself to *Gott*'s Hands in order to be able to care for Ella and Anna—and any more children they might be given. He found himself praying, deeply, honestly, and it brought renewal to his soul. He found himself looking down at Ella a few minutes later, now her husband, and he knew that he would treasure her so long as he had breath in his body.

By mutual understanding of Ella's delicate condition after giving birth, the honeymoon was postponed, but the *nacht* soon came when Ella approached Stephen with a determined gleam in her dark eyes . . .

Stephen caught her hands in his, then bent his head to kiss her fingers slowly, until he felt her impatience as she tried to get closer to him.

"Ella," he finally said. "It's only been a few weeks since Anna was born . . . I can't, we can't . . ."

"Six weeks." She smiled at him triumphantly. "I went to see May Miller and she said that was long enough to . . . heal . . . and that I could . . . we could . . ."

He laughed softly. "You actually talked with May about making love?" He delighted in her blush as she lifted her pert nose in the air and sniffed.

"Yes . . . I did."

"Well, then that deserves some action on my part, doesn't it?" He lifted his hands to her throat, then bent and kissed her with growing hunger. He loved her mouth with his tongue and teeth and lips and when she was breathing tiny sounds of pleasure, he slid his big hands down to cup her breasts. He squeezed gently, and she arched her back and moaned.

"You're more sensitive here now, aren't you?" he whispered.

She trembled as he withdrew his hand from her breast and she stared up at him with dazed eyes.

"Oh, Stephen . . ."

"I know, and I want to give you more pleasure, sweetheart."

She nodded and then reached for the pins on his blue shirt. She slid them out slowly and he grew impatient and started to help her. They both took his shirt off, revealing the taut muscles of his chest and the lean strength in his ribs. She found his own nipples with her soft fingertips and he closed his eyes against the wash of sensation that her touch produced.

"Does it feel good?" she asked and he managed a nod, then reached to find the pins that held her dress in place, and soon she was clad only in a brief shift, shivering with tension before him.

He reached for the hook and eye on the closure of his dark pants and eased them down while she watched, seemingly mesmerized. He knew his body was big, especially in its swollen state, and he wasn't sure that he could maintain control when she hesitantly touched him.

"How—is this going to work?" Her voice quavered as she reached out to him.

"*Ach*, Ella—it will," he promised as he lifted her and walked toward the bed. "It will . . ."

October advanced to its late stages with an abundance of good smells and color. Ella learned from the other Amish women in the community how to make homemade soft soap and how to bake pumpkin pies, and she was taking instruction from Joel Umble in the Old Order faith. Now, as she stretched to place a clothespin on a sheet on the line, she smiled to herself. She and Stephen continued to grow closer as husband and wife, in every way.

She hugged the secret feeling to herself and smiled warmly at Stephen when he came out of Dan's old cabin carrying Anna carefully in his arms. They had plans to expand the cabin in the spring, but for now, it proved the perfect love nest for the three of them.

"You look happy," Stephen said, a knowing warmth in the sea of his eyes.

"You would know, Mr. Lambert." She gave him a saucy

smile, then laughed out loud when he caught her close to his side even as he held the baby.

"Are you happy, Ella?" he asked softly as he stretched to nuzzle at her neck.

"Oh yes, Stephen," she whispered in return. "So very happy."

Anna burped loudly, breaking the rather serious moment, and they laughed out loud together.

"I've told you before," Stephen said once their laughter had faded, "that you have made me feel like I've found home, like I'm both back where I started in this place and forward looking at the same time, and I thank *Gott* every day for what we have."

"I do too," she agreed, nodding.

His handsome mouth curved into a knowing smile. "I know that troubles will *kumme*, but we will be able to face them together. And always, I want to celebrate a life of joy with you, Ella Lambert . . . Joy on Ice Mountain."

Please read on for a preview of
Kelly Long's next novel,

An Amish Wedding Feast on Ice Mountain!

Chapter One

The hot sunshine of the summer Thursday morning caught on the glassware and flower petals that gave special significance to the corner of the King kitchen where the *eck* table stood.

All that was needed was the bridal couple and their attendants to begin the special wedding feast where Jeb and Lucy King would receive the blessings and well wishes of both family and community.

But the wedding ceremony still went on, as it normally did, for a *gut* four hours, and Ransom King was bored. He let his gaze roam over the profile of his handsome big *bruder* and then paid brief attention to the sound of Bishop Umble's exhortation only to idly glance across the row at his fellow attendant and the one he was to escort for the day—Beth Mast.

The girl's plump cheeks were flushed a becoming pink and her small hands were clenched in her lap, as she sat, as attuned as a baby hare to every moment of her best friend's wedding. *I've never realized how pretty Beth is*, Ransom mused to himself but then something went subtly wrong. Beth's face drained of color and she wobbled slightly in her hard-backed chair.

She fell, like a wilting rose bud, slightly sideways, fast destined for the floor but Ransom was faster. He caught her neatly, ignoring the circle of whispers behind him, and pressed the back of his hand to her forehead as he lowered her with gentleness to the wooden floor. "Fainted only," he pronounced quietly, knowing Bishop Umble would probably continue with the ceremony whether one girl fainted or ten.

"She needs to eat," Ransom hissed over his shoulder, aware that the girl had been most likely too focused on her duties as attendant to have any breakfast. Someone handed him a morsel in a white cloth napkin. *Gut*, he thought. *Pie*. He pressed some blue crumbs to her lips and she opened her wide blue eyes in both dawning surprise and dismay.

"Blueberry pie . . . *ach*, my . . ."

Ransom smiled down at the intriguing freckles on her pert nose. "Oh, my, indeed."

"I have to get up," she whispered in visible desperation.

"Fine, but you're coming outside with me for a breath of fresh air," he muttered. "I'll wager the *gut* Bishop has about forty-five minutes left in him yet." He started to lift her and could tell she was about to protest. He bent his mouth to the delicate ear nearest him. "We don't want to make a scene, do we?"

Her gentle face flushed with new color as he drew her upright, catching her hand against the crook of his arm and escorting her down the open aisle between the amassed chairs with confident aplomb. It didn't matter to Ransom that there were titters of interest as they passed; he actually liked giving the older hens of his mountain community something to talk about. But as soon as he had Beth safely outside in the gentle breeze, he realized that the girl had no desire to make a spectacle of herself.

She drew her hand from his arm and swiped at her eyes. "I've ruined my best friend's wedding."

From another girl, the statement made might have been considered dramatic, but Beth's soft voice was subdued with sorrow that somehow struck a resonating chord in Ransom's usually immune heart. He sighed aloud then gently reached a hand to rub back and forth across her back, until he felt her spine stiffen.

She looked up at him with something akin to shock. "You're touching me."

He might have pointed out that he'd touched her when he'd helped her from the floor but instead he dropped his hand. He knew how conservative his Old Order Amish community could be. "Sorry. Reflex. Would you like a dipper of water before we *geh* back inside?"

She shook her head and a tendril of light brown hair escaped her *kapp* to curl becomingly about her cheek. He decided that she'd probably have a fit if he reached to fix it, so he offered his arm instead.

"*Kumme*," he murmured. "There's no ruined wedding— only a brief diversion and I'm glad to have been of service."

"*Danki*," she whispered, reaching a hesitant hand to his sleeve.

As her fingers settled on his arm, he decided with a strange certainty that Beth Mast was someone he wanted to know more than blueberry pie crumbs on pale lips and a soft back beneath light blue fabric. He escorted her inside and decided he must need something to eat himself for all that his mind was focused on the shy *maedel* by his side, but then he blinked and marched her purposely forward . . .

Beth stared down at the steaming plate of ham, mashed potatoes and gravy, corn, green beans, and cucumber relish that her stepmother, Viola, slid in front of her as she sat at the *eck*.

"You've got to eat, Beth—after that terrible fainting experience. My, people will think I don't feed you enough." Viola gave a soft laugh and drifted off into the crowd. Beth watched her go with wistful feelings of admiration.

Viola had been her stepmother since Beth was five. Beth's own *mamm* had died in a buggy accident before that and her *daed* always said that he had been blessed to meet Viola and her seven-year-old daughter, Rose. Beth knew her *daed* was right—that Viola was a blessing— especially since her *daed* passed away the previous year. Viola and Rose seemed to do all that they could to make sure Beth knew that she was an integral part of the running of the family's dairy farm, even though Beth grew tired sometimes.

Now she dutifully picked up her fork but made no effort to touch the plate. *No one would ever doubt I didn't have enough food as plump as I am* . . . But she pushed away this negative thought and began resolutely on the potatoes, anxious as always to please her stepmother. She jumped a moment later though when Lucy, the bride, leaned close to her.

"What did Ransom say to you outside, Beth?"

Her best friend's voice was a conspiratorial whisper

and Beth had to smile. "You're supposed to be concerned about your wedding day—and being Lucy King now."

Lucy shrugged her delicate shoulders and Beth watched her best friend's eyes sparkle with love for her new husband. "I know but I would also like to see you perhaps become part of the King family. Ransom is a catch."

Beth couldn't contain the blush that she knew heated her cheeks but she answered easily and without self-pity. "Which is exactly why he would never have eyes for me . . . Besides, he was just being kind."

"Well he's going to have to be 'kind' all of today. You know he's to be your escort for everything—oops, and here he comes now to sit by you." Beth almost giggled when Lucy withdrew and assumed a proper bridal expression.

"Are you feeling better?" Ransom asked low as he maneuvered his long legs around the chair and under the table. He set a loaded plate on the place in front of him and gave her what appeared to be an intent look.

She swallowed a bit. "I—I'm fine. *Danki*. And thank you for being so kind in helping me . . . I should have eaten this morning." She glanced at her fast cooling plate and the mound of food but couldn't work up an appetite with Ransom in such close proximity.

He had such a reputation with the girls and even Rose, her beautiful older stepsister, had often spoken of him with feminine interest. Beth could understand why . . . His brown hair was stroked with lighter shades of blond and his dark brown eyes were soulful and curious. He had a commanding profile and soothing presence which immediately put a girl at ease—except Beth wasn't feeling easy at the moment. He'd turned from his plate and studied her with apparent interest.

"Well, I know why you didn't eat. Like as not, you were doing what I was doing—couldn't even have a forkful of scrambled eggs because I was so busy helping Jeb get ready."

Beth heard the warmth in his voice when he mentioned his older *bruder*. She knew there were six years between the King *buwes*—Jeb at twenty-six and Ransom at twenty.

"You—you must love him very much," she said shyly.

Ransom smiled, a casual lift of his lips that produced a dimple in his cheek and made Beth think of an errant little boy. "*Ach*, I do—of course. And I'll miss him though he'll only be down the road at Lucy's place."

"Will he work at the woodshop as well as farming?" she asked, setting down her fork on the white tablecloth.

Ransom shrugged. "Probably. Especially if he needs more money when the *kinner* start to come."

Beth swallowed, feeling her face flame. Rarely had she known a man to be so matter-of-fact about the appearance of children and she wasn't sure how to respond.

"Put a foot wrong, didn't I?" Ransom laughed low. "I apologize."

"*Nn—nee*," she protested feebly. "It's fine."

"How *auld* are you, if I might ask, Beth Mast?"

She sighed, wishing she could be witty and charming somehow. "I'm twenty." *And everyone in the community probably thinks I'll die an* auld *maid. . . .*

But she'd noticed that Ransom had raised his small punch glass in one of his big hands. "Then here's to us being twenty together."

She grabbed her glass, sloshing it a bit over her hand but then carefully clinked her glass against his and put the strawberry punch to her lips. She'd never had anyone offer a toast in her direction and the feeling was heady.

"To us," she murmured, watching his tan throat work as he swallowed. And suddenly, her day took on a rare hue of promise.

Chapter Two

As dusk set in and the fireflies began to dance, Ransom eased the curry brush down the side of the faithful horse, Benny, and let his thoughts drift back over the day's wedding. Beth Mast had proved a charming companion for all of the games and visiting that went on and he'd found himself studying her discreetly on more than one occasion.

"You almost done, *sohn*?"

Ransom looked up as his father came into the barn and set a lantern down on a barrel top.

"*Jah*, Daed. I was thinking more than working, truth to tell."

"Well, it'll be strange not to have Jeb in the *haus*, that's for sure."

"Uh—right."

"Not what you were thinking of?" His *fater*'s voice was warm. "Perhaps it was the bevy of young *maedels* there today? Or one in particular?"

"*Nee*," Ransom laughed. "No one special."

"So I won't be gaining another *dochder*-in-law anytime soon?"

Ransom put down the brush and went over to lay a gentle arm round his *daed*'s shoulders. The older man had recovered from a heart attack recently and sometimes seemed more fragile than Ransom cared to acknowledge.

"No, Daed. If there's ever any girl I *kumme* to love, I promise you'll be the first—or somewhere in the top three—who *kummes* to know it."

They laughed together and then headed for the *haus* in the gloaming of the evening. Once there, Ransom sat down to the table to enjoy a cold supper of stewed tomatoes and sugar, egg salad, hearty bacon, and broccoli salad with a blueberry cake for after.

His *mamm* was quiet, obviously tired after a day's helping at the wedding, and Ransom gently patted her shoulder as he got up to take his dishes to the sink. He bent and kissed her soft cheek, balancing his plate in his left hand. "*Danki*, Mamm—for all of your hard work. I know Jeb and Lucy appreciate it."

"As well they should," his sister Esther mumbled sourly, her irritability bearing witness to her own tiredness.

Ransom laughed. "*Kumme* on, Esther. You know you loved every minute of it."

"Better watch out, Ransom King," Esther quipped. "Or you're going to get trapped into a wedding of your own one of these days—especially after the way you chase the girls around."

She got up from the table and swatted at him with a damp dishtowel. He easily evaded her then jumped up to sit on the counter, swinging his legs. "You be older than I, Esther . . . Isn't it time you yourself were, uh, trapped as you put it."

His sister glared at him. Everyone knew that Esther was moody and scared off any prospective suitors with her sharp tongue but Ransom still thought she was beautiful—even if a bit off-putting. But now, she marched from the kitchen, obviously dismissing him in a fit.

"Ransom, you shouldn't tease her so," his *mamm* said in soft rebuke as she began to gather the plates to wash.

"I know," he grinned. "But it's too much fun to stop."

"Well, while you're having fun, I need you to remember that I want you to take some Lamb's Ear plantings over to Viola Mast's *haus* tomorrow. She asked for them special today and you need to also return the tables we borrowed."

Ransom jumped down from the sink and headed for the stairs with a yawn. "No problem, *maam. Gut nacht.*"

He expected to drop right off to sleep but instead found himself tossing uncomfortably while strange images of Beth Mast and ripe blueberries played at the back of his mind.

Dawn had yet to stretch its pink fingers across the summer morning sky when Beth slipped quietly from her bed. She was grateful for the feel of Thumbelina, her large Maine Coon Cat, when he brushed against her legs in the inky darkness. She dressed with hasty hands, anxious to get the milking done that was needed for breakfast. Friday meant doing the laundry—always a prodigious task, but by way of the soiled tablecloths that Viola had loaned and brought back from the King's, it became a monstrous chore.

But Beth was undaunted; she understood that work was a necessary thing in life. And, as her step*mamm* often said, "The more time spent in work, the less there was for idle thought." Beth knew she had a tendency to let her mind wander, so she was happy for the often heavy chores.

Thumbelina prowled ahead of her as she left her third-floor room and made her way down the stairs, careful to avoid the steps she knew that creaked in an effort not to wake her step*mamm* and Rose. The two had large rooms on the second floor of the *auld* farm*haus*, and, as was typical, they each had placed a mound of clothes and linens outside their respective doors the *nacht* before so that Beth might gather their laundry without causing them to wake before breakfast was ready.

She balanced the tall pile of clothes and walked blind down the last set of stairs to the first floor. The wash room was adjacent to the kitchen—a cramped space, barely big enough to hold the wringer washer, large tub, and then—when needed, the ironing board and heavy irons heated on the woodstove. She had to go outside, through a narrow back door, to pump the water, but she understood Viola not wanting her to use the kitchen pump and possibly sloshing water on the hickory hardwoods.

It took five pails of water to get the metal tub at a *gut* level for washing, and she hastily separated the whites from the colors after lugging the buckets inside. She plunged the first of Rose's dark aprons into the water, watching the fabric balloon up then squashing it down once more. She continued through dresses of different hues then paused for a moment to catch the breeze from the back open door only to hear Thumbelina let out a piercing meow.

Beth jumped in spite of herself then stepped outside in time to see Ransom King driving a wagon slowly down the lane that led to the barn. He gave her a casual wave and she lifted her hand, feeling a strange pounding in her chest. She was suddenly very conscious of the perspiration stains under her arms and the fact that her dark hair had escaped her *kapp* in errant tendrils.

"He must be returning the tables to the barn from the wedding," she muttered to Thumbelina who purred loudly in return. "And he probably won't even stop at the *haus* . . ."

Still, she grasped her hair with ruthless fingers and hastily pinned it back as best she could then returned with a resolute effort to the chore of the washing. She was working the wringer washer when a male voice sounded from the doorway and Thumbelina's purring increased.

"That's a big cat."

Beth spun then swallowed hard, careless of the dripping water from the pillowcase she held.

"Uh . . . *jah* . . . His name is Thumbelina. I—I thought he was a girl at first and then . . ." She floundered helplessly, wishing she could be as beautiful and confident as her older stepsister.

Ransom smiled and stooped down to rub his hand in the thick gray fur of the animal and Beth had the irreverent memory of his stroking her back on the previous day.

"I came over to put the tables in the barn, all right?" He slanted a glance up at her through thick lashes and she wet her lips.

"*Jah*, do you need any help?"

He rose and shook his head. "*Nee*—it's men's work anyway."

"*Ach*, I'm as strong as an ox," Beth returned in a cheery tone, unconsciously repeating what Viola often said.

She watched him as he let his dark eyes skim down her damp frame and up again. He shook his head. "I don't know who's been putting such ideas in your head, but whoever they are—they're wrong. You look like you should be cutting flowers not doing such heavy labor as this." He gestured to the wash piles, visible inside the door. "Where's your stepsister to help?"

Beth drank in the kindness of his words and then snapped back to the moment. "*Ach*, Rose is delicate—a doctor told her long ago that she should only do light tasks as she tends to faint . . ."

Ransom gave her a wry look that she couldn't quite understand. "Uh-huh," he said, then reached out to gently tug the wet pillowcase from her fingers. "What do you say to the two of us getting this job done faster?"

Beth stared at him, appalled. "I couldn't—couldn't let you help me."

He put his hands on his lean hips, ignoring the dripping cloth he held. "And why not? I've wrung things out for Mamm plenty of times . . . *Kumme*, let me show you."

She watched helplessly as his light blue shirt became even more soaked as he took charge of the wringer and soon had the clothes flying through.

"Can you hang these on the clothesline?" he asked over his shoulder and she hurried to help.

She was stretching to place the last wooden clothespin when she heard Rose's voice and spun in dismay, thinking desperately of a way to explain Ransom King washing women's dresses.

Chapter Three

Beth wanted to dissolve into a spot on the clean grass, but instead she swallowed and walked over to the small wash room. Rose stood like some kind of fairy apparition in the doorway; the sunlight playing off her magnificent red hair, which hung unbound down to her hips. She also was wearing her dressing gown but was standing with visible confidence as Ransom stood, paused, with a dripping cloth in his hands.

"What's going on this fine morning, Beth?" Rose's voice was high and breathy and Beth ignored the blatant fact that any other girl would have run back to her room if caught in such a state, with her hair loose, as only a husband should see it. But not her Rose . . . *Nee*, Rose has confidence and innocence, Beth thought with pride.

"*Ach* . . . Ransom offered to help with the washing and I . . ."

"Let him, of course," Rose smiled. "What kindness, so early in the morning. You must *kumme* in and have some breakfast, Ransom. I'm sure all of this work has made you hungry."

Beth watched Ransom wring out the towel he held and

then look up at her stepsister. *Heavens only know what he's thinking . . . Surely he must be floored by Rose's beauty while I look like. . . .*

"Breakfast would be nice," Ransom said. "You go on and cook while Beth and I finish here."

Beth hastened to intervene. "*Ach*, but I do the cooking. I'm sorry, Rose—I forgot breakfast with the pile of laundry and—"

Rose waved a delicate hand in dismissal. "I'll cook, Beth. Please *kumme* in, Ransom, and dry off. Beth's *gut* at the washing—she's used to it. Besides, I wanted to talk about you making a new spice box for the kitchen—a surprise for my *mamm*'s birthday."

Beth grabbed the towel from Ransom's hand. "*Jah*, please *geh*. I'm fine here."

She felt him give her a measuring glance then finally he nodded. "All right. If you're sure."

She watched them enter the *haus* single file through the narrow door and then Rose gently closed the wood, leaving Beth standing, feeling appropriately shut out of any such intimacies as morning conversation and flowing hair. She turned with a resolute face back to the washer and tried to ignore Thumbelina's plaintive meow.

"Well," she said, finally looking at the cat. "That was that."

Ransom knew he had a reputation for being a flirt but the overt manner in which Rose Mast paraded about the kitchen in her dressing gown made him long to run back outside. He wondered rather uneasily where Frau Mast was as Rose reached over his damp shoulder to gain the salt shaker for the scrambled eggs she was making.

"Uh . . . I could cook, if you'd like to—get dressed," he said finally.

But Rose appeared oblivious to her hair and attire and waved airily at him. "*Ach*, I'm quite comfortable, Ransom. But you must be feeling damp in that shirt. Why don't you—"

Ransom was spared any suggestion on the girl's part when Viola Mast entered the room from the staircase but apparently didn't notice him seated at the table.

"Rose, whatever are you doing? You know it's Beth's job to cook. Where is that laz—" With a start, she caught sight of him. "—I mean . . . girl?"

Ransom watched Viola change facial expressions as fast as a shadow slips out of the sunlight. And he felt troubled. There was something going on in this *haus* of women that made him worry for Beth. *Not that it's any of my business. . . .*

Viola continued. "Why Ransom King—I didn't see you there. Rose, dear, run along and dress and I'll check if Beth needs any help and take over here."

"*Ach*, Mamm, I'm fine. Don't be so stuffy. Ransom's seen a woman's hair before, I'm sure."

He didn't respond to the loaded comment but rubbed absently at his wet sleeve.

Viola took the moment into her own hands with a none-too-subtle pinch to Rose's arm. "I must insist Rose. Now, *sei se gut.*"

Rose flounced to the stairs with a smiling backward glance in his direction then he rose from the table bench. "I'll *geh* help Beth finish the washing while you cook, Frau Mast."

He didn't know how Viola might have responded because Beth emerged from the wash room.

"Ah, there you are, child," Viola practically cooed.

"*Kumme* sit down with our guest and have something to eat. You must have been up quite early."

Ransom didn't miss the surprise on Beth's sweet face and then the flush of happiness. "*Danki*, Viola . . . *Danki* for getting breakfast and I'd love to sit down but I'd better *geh* and change."

Ransom cleared his throat. "You wouldn't be the only wet one at the table."

She looked at him, with her wide blue eyes, and he was reminded of a baby owl peeking out from its nest. He smiled at the thought and delighted in her return smile, but Viola didn't seem as pleased.

"The eggs are ready now, child. I'm sorry, Ransom— Beth must indeed change, as is only proper."

He sighed to himself then pulled a pocket watch from his hip pocket. "Well, now that I look at the time, I'd best be getting back to the wood shop. I left the Lamb's Ear plantings that you wanted in a box on the front porch. I'd love breakfast another time. *Danki*, ladies." He turned and made for the front door, but not before he'd given a last lingering look at Beth's face.

"You simply must finish up the breakfast—I'm having those pesky chest pains again," Viola said. "You may change later. I'll *geh* and sit in Rose's room and you may serve us there."

Beth murmured a reply, still thinking about the fact that Ransom King had helped her do the wash when Viola paused on the bottom stair step. "*Ach*, and Beth, perhaps you don't understand what's proper with young men— you've had so little experience . . . But a *maedel* does not let a man help her with such menial chores as the laundry. It is not fitting."

Beth bit her lip, thinking of Rose in her dressing gown, but then nodded. "*Jah*, Viola. It won't happen again."

"*Gut*. I'm glad to hear it." Viola disappeared up the steps and Beth bowed her head. It was a shame that it would never happen again—she'd rather enjoyed working side by side with Ransom King.

He's nice . . . she thought then hurried to salvage the burning toast.

Twenty minutes later, she hefted a loaded tray of crisp bacon, scrambled eggs, grilled tomatoes, toast, and home-made marmalade up the stairs and managed a soft knock on Rose's door.

Rose bade her enter and Beth got the door open, balancing the tray on her hip. Neither Viola nor Rose looked up when she got the tray into the room and started to set it up on the small table by the window, reserved for such occasions.

Rose popped off the bed, now suitably dressed with her hair *kapp*ed and snatched a piece of bacon from a plate. Beth watched her in some dismay, knowing that no grace had been given for the food. But Viola seemed willing to overlook the infraction as she calmly took a place at the table.

"That will be all, Beth. *Danki*."

Beth nodded, preparing to leave the room when her stepmother's voice gave her pause. "*Ach*, and Beth, I know you planned on attending the blueberry frolic to-morrow, but I'm afraid that I must *geh* to chaperone, of course, and that black-faced goat of yours is about due for a late lambing. Someone should watch her."

Beth felt her heart sink. The blueberry frolic was one of the social highlights of the summer but she couldn't deny that Cleo had been showing signs of being near to giving birth and she might need help.

"Viola, perhaps Jimmy Stolfus could stay with her." Jimmy was the twelve-year-old *buwe* who'd been hired to help Beth about the farm.

She watched Viola smile. "Now dear, you know couldn't possibly know that I gave Jimmy the day off tomorrow, and besides, Rose will bring you back some berries for jam. Won't you, Rose?"

"Mmmm-hmmm," Rose mumbled, her pretty mouth full.

Beth nodded her thanks and left the room, closing the door quietly behind her. It's of no matter, she told herself stoutly. *I probably wouldn't have had too* gut *a time anyway.* But then, Ransom King's smiling face danced behind her eyes and she had to push the thought away with deliberation before heading back downstairs to clean the kitchen.

More from Bestselling Author
JANET DAILEY

More by Bestselling Author
Hannah Howell

31901063898136